Two Times Two

HEARTLINES

Books by Pam Lyons

A Boy Called Simon
He Was Bad
It Could Never Be ...
Latchkey Girl
Danny's Girl

Books by Anita Eires

Tug Of Love
Summer Awakening
Spanish Exchange
Star Dreamer
Californian Summer

Books by Mary Hooper

Love Emma XXX
Follow That Dream
My Cousin Angie

Books by Barbara Jacobs

Two Times Two

Books by Jane Pitt

Loretta Rose

Books by Ann de Gale

Island Encounter

Heartlines

Barbara Jacobs

Two Times Two

A Pan Original

First published 1984 by Pan Books Ltd,
Cavaye Place, London SW10 9PG

9 8 7 6 5 4 3

© Barbara Jacobs 1984

ISBN 0 330 28492 4

Phototypeset by Input Typesetting Ltd, London
Printed in Great Britain by
Richard Clay Ltd, Bungay, Suffolk

Chapter 1

The coffee bar on the first floor was thumping to the music of the roller disco below. My nose tightened against the familiar mixture of smells – chlorine from the swimming pool, sweaty plimsolls, hot dogs and onions – as I pushed through the crowds of kids in track suits, leotards and shorts. The Leisure Centre, our old haunt, hadn't changed a bit. And why should it in only five weeks? Still, it felt like a lifetime, perhaps because, in that five weeks away on holiday, my whole life had changed. Miraculously. And I had to find Kim to tell her all about it.

'Hi!' I yelled across the music at Marie. She was sitting at our usual table, among the mess of empty plastic cups and paper plates, her unmistakable red-gold mop of hair shaking as she bounced absent-mindedly to the latest disco hit.

'Hi, Joanne! Stranger! Look, what d'you reckon to my tan, then? Stick your arm out. Come on. Put it against mine. There! . . . Hey, how come five weeks of mingey Brighton sun equals two scorching weeks in Benidorm? I paid good money for this tan. It ought to be better than yours. Don't speak to me now, Joanne Farmer. I'm sulking!' she bubbled, pretending to be all put out.

'Seen Kim?' I grinned, settling into the chair opposite. Maybe Kim was at the roller-disco. That would explain why she hadn't been round at our house as soon as our car pulled in. She was always there, waiting to hear the news about my holiday. But this time . . .

'Kim?' Marie shrugged. 'No. But I can't honestly say I've been looking for her. Only got back from holiday yesterday myself. Ellen'll be up here in a minute, though. She's still changing from badminton. I said I'd come up and get the coffees in, but look at that queue!'

'Roller disco. Wish I'd known. I was wondering if Kim'd come to it . . .'

'Not exactly Kim's scene, is it? Especially not now!' Marie frowned.

'What d'you mean by that?' I asked.

Something was wrong. I could feel it. When you've been best mates with someone for as long as I'd been mates with Kim, you get this kind of sixth sense about each other. I'd got it almost as soon as we arrived home. Without Kim there, the news about Tony and me had lost some of its fizz. And the excitement I'd felt was being replaced by a niggling worry.

All along I'd wondered if Kim would be OK on her own, this summer. She didn't seem to get on so well with any of the others. They all felt sorry for her, true enough, since she'd lost her brother in that accident last year. But they had no patience with her quiet withdrawn ways. Moody, they said she was.

'Oh, Ellen said something about Kim having a

boyfriend. Kim's been shouting her mouth off about some big romance for the last week or so. Can't say I believe it, really. Not Kim . . . but, while we're on the subject of boys, I've got to tell you about this guy I met in Benidorm, well, on the plane, actually. Not that I fell in love with him on the plane going out, 'cos you don't, do you? They all look like little white slugs till they've been in the sun for a few days, but this Norman . . .'

'Norman?!' I exploded.

'Forget the name, remember the frame! He was built like a cross-Channel swimmer when he pulled his t-shirt off by the pool. Honest. There was this crowd of girls from Birmingham, and they all did a dead faint on to their sun-loungers when they saw him. Six foot three of solid British muscle, he was! Can you imagine that with a tan on it, and this sun-streaked blond hair and one of those wide even grins that you read about in magazines and always hope you'll bump into one day? Jo, when he looked at me, and grinned, I nearly died. It was the black bikini that did it . . .

'Yours or his?' I asked.

She thumped me, giggling.

'Let me tell the story. All you've got to do is listen and keep your mouth glued up,' she said.

I kept my mouth glued, and pretended I was listening. But I was wondering. Marie's stories were always good value, unless you had other things on your mind, as I had just then.

Kim, for a start. Kim with a boyfriend. I couldn't imagine it. Not just yet. I'd been trying to build up her confidence slowly, by bringing her here to the Leisure Centre, and introducing her to one or two of the boys on the badminton team. She'd started to relax a little, because I wasn't out chasing everything that looked like a cross-Channel swimmer. For years, Tony had been the only one for me.

Tony. Marie always said I was crazy to keep that old childhood romance going. But every year there was Brighton, and every year, there was Tony, growing up from gawky best friend to . . . something more. Much, much more.

I shivered with happiness, just remembering.

'Yeah, that's exactly what I did when he pulled me towards him on the beach, Joanne. You know, I couldn't catch my breath. All we needed was a couple of violins to go with the sea and the moonlight, and we could've been starring in a film. It *was* for my story, that little shiver, wasn't it?' Marie asked, doubtfully. 'Or is that far-away look in your eye for *your* big holiday romance? And don't tell me who with. Let me guess! You're the faithful type, aren't you, Jo?'

'Has she got her "I love Tony" face on?' Ellen asked, coming up behind us, through the crush. 'How did the holiday go? And have you heard all about Norm, Manchester's answer to Marie's prayers?'

I grinned. Ellen was a bit easier to take than Marie, calmer, quietly sarky, but funny with it.

'Where's the coffee?' she asked, searching among the empty cups.

'Just going to get in the queue, wasn't I, Jo? But I

was up to the moonlight scene on the beach, and I didn't want to spoil it,' Marie spluttered, scraping out of her chair, and making for the queue at the counter.

Ellen's eyebrows arched under her dark fringe.

'There's six more big scenes to come!' she sighed. 'And the killer's the one in the baggage-handling room at the airport back home where he says they won't spoil the romance by keeping in touch, but he'll probably be there next year! Marie always falls for them, doesn't she? Whatever makes you happy, that's what I say! You, too, eh? I mean, anyone can see you're bursting with some good news about Tony.'

Marie slopped back with the coffee, trying to keep the beat of the music while carrying three plastic cups. She was losing the battle. She slammed all three on the table and waggled her hands around to cool them.

'What're you two looking so smug about?' she asked.

'Jo's about to tell us some big news!' Ellen smiled, sitting opposite me and leaning forward on her elbows. 'Go on. Surprise me!' she said.

Marie flopped down, too. Ellen had been right. I *was* bursting with the news. But I hadn't really wanted to tell it here, not with disco music blaring out, and the screams of crazy kids from the swimming pool interrupting my hazy happiness. I'd wanted to tell it from the beginning, to Kim, who knew exactly how I felt, and exactly what this was going to mean to me.

9

'Go on, then!' Marie urged, impatiently.

'Tony's coming to art college. Here,' I said, letting all the happiness out.

'Wow!' Ellen breathed. 'So it *is* the Real Thing!'

'Aw, come on. I had twenty-seven real things last year, and you weren't half that impressed!' Marie complained, jokingly.

'This is different. Joanne's been going out with Tony every summer since she was . . . how old?' Ellen asked.

'Ten . . .' I murmured.

'And it's lasted!' Ellen said, all amazed.

'So? Maybe Norm and I'll go on for ever, too. Happily ever after, in Benidorm . . .' Marie murmured dreamily.

'Tell us more! What happened? What's *going* to happen? You getting engaged or anything? He could've gone anywhere to art college, couldn't he? Even stayed in Brighton. I'm dying to meet him. What's he like?' Ellen asked.

'Oh, sort of nice. Like a best mate, really,' I murmured, knowing I was telling it all wrong. But I didn't have the time, or the right sort of audience to tell it like it really was. Magic. Very special. Perfect. 'He's tallish, with mousey-coloured hair, and the most fantastic eyes and smile. He blushes a lot, but he really feels things, and . . .'

No. It sounded wimpish. And that's not what Tony was like at all. But how do you say, in words, out loud, what one pair of greenish-bluish eyes can do to you, when they look into yours, with just a hint of a smile, and the whole world slips into the distance, and there's only the two of you left, without words, just with feelings that both of you understand?

'Hmm. The sensitive type. 'Course, he would be, being an artist, an' all,' Marie started jabbering. 'I knew an art student once. His name was Rolf. He wasn't English, but I can't remember where he came from, anyway, this night he said to me, "I'd like to paint your hair. It's such a beautiful colour". I thought that was pretty sensitive. But crazy. All art students 're crazy, if you ask me!'

'Tony's not crazy. He's ordinary,' I muttered. 'Ask Kim. She's seen a photograph of him. She's even talked to him on the phone. She was round at our house when he rang up, once. She . . . she liked him . . . D'you know where she is tonight, Ellie?'

'Search me. She's gone a bit funny since she started seeing this guy she's going out with,' Ellen said, off-handedly.

'What d'you mean, funny? And who is he? Where'd she meet him?' I asked.

'Well . . . I dunno, of course, 'cos Kim and I aren't exactly close friends, but from what I can make out, she went to him to get her hair done and . . .'

'He's a hairdresser?' I groaned.

'And he's got some weird ideas, I reckon. I bumped into Kim in town last week, and she started laying down the law to me, telling me that I ought to pull myself together, and take myself more seriously, and all this rubbish. She was talking like a television programme, not like her at all. Seems this guy's a lot older than her, and dead sophisticated. I've never met him. No one has. He's Italian. Paolo, she said his name was,' Ellen sneered.

'Doesn't sound like Kim at all!' I murmured, shaking my head.

'If you ask me, which you don't, but I'll tell you anyway, you want to let Kim go her own way now, Jo. She's never really been one of the crowd. She's heading for trouble if she carries on like this,' Marie said.

It sounded odd, coming from Marie.

'Trouble?' I asked.

'Wait till you see her. You'll know what I mean!' Marie murmured. She looked at me, dead straight, without a trace of her usual light-hearted bubbling. 'She's changed. Ellen's not coming right out and saying it, 'cos she knows she's your best mate. But I'm saying it. You won't like her now. None of us do. And that's the truth.'

There was a lull in the music from the roller disco, and a tense silence between the three of us. All the shivery excitement I'd felt drained out of me. I didn't believe Marie or Ellen.

'I'll find out for myself,' I said tightly. 'I'll go home. Maybe she's called.'

Marie and Ellen glanced at each other quickly.

'Don't get us wrong, Joanne,' Ellen murmured.

'OK. It's OK,' I smiled weakly, getting up to leave.

If something was wrong with Kim, I felt responsible. She relied on me so heavily, and maybe I'd never realized how much I relied on her to listen to my stories about Tony. Should I have gone away for all that time, and left her to fend for herself?

On the way home I found myself remembering the times when she'd sat in our front room, half listening to my records, trying not to cry while I'd told her that some day she'd find a boyfriend of her own, someone like Tony, and that then everything would change.

'You think so? You really think so?' she'd asked, desperately.

Well, now she had. And she'd changed. Who was I to be jealous or worried? It was her own life, and she was entitled to all the happinesss she could get, no matter what Marie and Ellen said.

'Any news from Kim? Did she phone?' I asked Mum as soon as I walked in through our back door.

'No, love. Just Tony. He phoned to see if we'd got home safely. He was a bit disappointed that you were out, but I said you'd gone to look for Kim. You didn't find her, then?'

I shook my head.

'She'll be round tomorrow. She always comes on Sundays!' Mum reassured me.

But she didn't. And when I called, her dad said that she'd gone out for the day in her boyfriend's car, but that she'd probably call for me, as usual, the next day, the first day of term.

For the first time in my life, I felt as if Kim was shutting me out. How many times had she felt like that in the past, when I'd raved on and on about Tony? It was worth thinking about. But it didn't help, much.

Chapter 2

I woke before the alarm and glanced at the clock. It was half past six. The September sunlight filtered through the curtains, and it took me a few seconds to remember that I was home, and not in our rented cottage at Brighton.

Half past six had been the time I'd woken there, each morning, before Mum and Dad stirred. I'd pulled on my jeans and my Snoopy sweatshirt, gulped down a cup of coffee in the tiny beamed kitchen, and raced out, through the maze of cobbled streets just off the sea front, to the café where Tony would be waiting for me.

It was the only café in town open at that time in the morning, and a few yawning bus-drivers and market stall-holders would be there, droopy-eyed over hot buttered toast, or bacon and eggs. Only the idiots were out at that hour. Idiots, and kids in love.

All through the rest of the day we'd be surrounded by Tony's mates, hassled into picnics and games of football on the beach, boat-trips and slot-machine sessions, dragged into folk clubs and discos, hustled into parties. But the time between seven and ten in the morning was ours, just ours, to be alone in, to speak only when we wanted to, to be very close.

Most mornings we walked along the pebbly beach, or along the path beneath the cliffs, Tony carrying his sketch book and pencils, holding my hand, always looking with his eyes half-closed at things I missed: a boat out at sea; squabbling seagulls on the shore;

an old man searching the beach for pennies under the pier; things to think about or to paint. And often, almost without my realizing it, those half-closed eyes would be focused on my face, and I'd turn and catch his glance and squeeze his hand more tightly.

It had been a morning like that when he'd told me about the art college. It was the day before I left, and there was a mistiness that morning over the sea like all the tears I wanted to cry. This time, I didn't want to leave.

'I've had a letter, Joanne,' he'd murmured, tucking his sketch book under his arm so that he could reach into his pocket. 'Sit down, and I'll read it to you.'

I sat in the shingle at the edge of the lacy waves.

'Dear Mr Mercer,' he read. 'Your application has been successful. We can offer you a place on the Foundation Course in Art and Design at the above college.'

'Which college?' I'd asked, all excited that he'd been successful somewhere.

'This college,' he smiled, waggling the letter in front of me.

I stared, unable to speak, swallowing back the lump in my throat as I read the name of our City Art College on the top of the letter.

'Well. . .?' he asked, finally.

'You never said. . .you never said you were applying there!' I breathed.

'I didn't want to. Might've raised your hopes, or might've sent them crashing down. I'm not sure, not completely sure, whether it's what you'd want me to do. Are you ready for this, for more of me?'

Tears tumbled down my face. I flung my arms round his neck, and cried and cried.

'Is that yes or no?' he laughed nervously into my damp hair.

'Yes!' I sobbed. 'Yes, yes, yes! Yes, I'm ready, no, I can't believe it, and yes, it can't happen soon enough. Are you sure it's what you want, too?'

'Did I forget to tell you I love you?' he whispered, lifting my chin in his cupped palm, so that I looked into his eyes that were the colour of the misty distance where sea and sky met.

'I love you too, Tony,' I whispered back.

Love in a mist, touched by sunshine, that's what it had always been. Now, the sun would shine for ever and ever. Now, we'd never need those long painful weeks of phone calls and letters and missing each other. . .

The alarm rang, jolting me out of memories.

'Joanne!' my Mum's voice shouted up the stairs. 'Quarter past seven. School!'

Even that didn't sound as bad as it usually did. Now, I had a few dreams to hold on to, a little breathing-space before they came true.

But there was Kim to face yet, I thought, as I examined my sleepy morning expression in the bath-room mirror. And then I shook myself.

'Don't be stupid!' my mind told my furrowed eyebrows. 'Kim's been your best friend as long as you can remember. Do you honestly reckon that one guy's going to change all that? What do Marie and Ellen know anyway?'

16

I smiled, dunked my face in the warm water, and came up, still smiling. I was sure everything was going to work out just fine.

'Jo! Do I have to come up there and drag you down to eat this so-called nourishing breakfast you made me buy for you?' Mum shouted up at me.

'Coming! I'm coming!' I yelled through the bathroom door.

Mum didn't think much of my passion for muesli. Actually, it was Tony who'd got me on to eating it, and wholemeal bread, and bean-shoot salads. He liked crazy food, and there was plenty of it about in Brighton. Just the taste of that muesli took me back. . . Four days ago. Only four days ago. . . And only three weeks or so to wait for him!

Kim's banging at the back door brought me to my senses. I leapt out of the chair, flung open the door, and hugged her, all excitedly.

'Kim! Fantastic! Can't wait to tell you all my news. It's great to see you. Hang on a sec while I get my bag. What d'you reckon, then? How do I look? Fit and bursting with happiness?' I bubbled.

Kim stiffened, and took a tiny step backwards. But I noticed it. And then I noticed her.

Funny, you can be really close to someone, thinking you're looking at them, and not really see them at all. I'd run up and hugged Kim, without noticing that she didn't look anything like the Kim I remembered, the shy blushing kid I'd always thought of as a younger sister.

She looked taller, slimmer. Her hair was cut into

a gleaming bob, streaked with pale gold, and her eyes, always wide and scared-looking, were outlined in pale blue pencil. For school?

'Kim. . .' I stammered. 'Just look at you! You look. . .'

'Better? Yeah, I know. Get a move on, Jo. It's almost twenty past.'

Her face registered none of the delight I felt at seeing her again. She just glanced impatiently at her watch and tapped her foot, didn't even step inside. Suddenly I felt gawky and all over the place. I pushed my tangle of hair behind my ears, took my bag from the chair, and stumbled out to join her.

I had a job keeping up with her. She had shiny patent pumps on, with a little heel that clicked as she walked very tall, looking ahead, and there was a tightness round the edges of her mouth that I'd never seen before.

'Are you mad with me about something?' I stammered.

'No. Why? Should I be?' she asked, with a strange laugh.

'It's just that you don't seem to want to talk. . .' I mumbled.

'Jo, you're the one who talks. Remember? And I suppose you want to talk about Tony? So carry on. Carry on. I'm listening.'

'I don't think you are,' I grumbled.

She stopped in her clicking little walk and looked me up and down.

'Don't you think it's about time you listened to me?' she asked.

I gulped, and nodded. I'd never seen Kim in this sort of mood before. She was sure of herself, as I'd never been, never once. There was a sort of poise to her. Except that it didn't quite seem to fit her. Somewhere, lurking behind that slightly bored expression I was sure was the old Kim, the one who'd never said boo to a goose, let alone me.

'Here's the bus. Jump on, and I'll let you into the secret,' she smiled, as if she had some private joke going on inside her.

'What secret?' I hissed, as I scrambled on to the platform untangling my bag from the bus door.

She waited until we'd found a seat.

'I'm in love,' she murmured, dramatically.

'Me, too! And guess what? Tony's coming! Here! In three weeks time! He's coming to the art college, and Kim...' I added, warned by the narrowing of her eyes that she was annoyed that I'd interrupted her news, her moment of glory '...that means that we can make up foursomes, you and me, and Tony and your boyfriend, maybe doubles for badminton or go to Boogy's disco, or just sit round playing records and...'

'No,' she said, decisively. 'No. I don't think Paolo would like that. In fact I know he wouldn't. Your trouble, Jo, is that you think everyone's like your Tony, sort of young and sweet and big-brotherly, and interested in going round with the gang to that scruffy Leisure Centre. It's not Paolo's scene. And to be honest, it's not mine, either. I'm past that stage now, thank goodness!'

'What stage?'

'Well. . .the boy and girl stage, I think you'd call it, the gang stage. I've found something different.'

I couldn't believe this was Kim talking, talking down to me, talking as if I was still in white ankle socks with two slides in my hair and a gap where my front teeth ought to be. She had her mouth all scrunched up like someone advertising the right way to eat an extra strong mint.

I wasn't going to let it get me down. I wasn't. If Kim was going to act up, then I was going to act normal. Sooner or later she was going to have to climb down.

'Look, this is me, your old mate Jo,' I laughed. 'So tell me, what's different about love? I love Tony. You love this Paolo bloke. Fair enough. We've got something in common. It's the same fantastic feeling!'

'Oh, is it?' she sneered, standing up and smoothing her skirt down as the bus pulled up outside school.

'Course it is!' I huffed.

'It's not,' she said.

We clambered off the bus together, me all arms and lanky legs, Kim almost elegantly.

'You see, this is a kind of certain feeling that I've never had before. I don't want anyone else. I don't need anyone else. I don't need Ellen, with her sarky digs, or stupid Marie. And, sorry about this, Jo, but I don't really need you, either. Nothing personal. And I'm not saying we can't be friends any more, or anything like that. But this is private, what there is between me and Paolo. It's only for two people. I'm finished with kids' stuff like cheap discos and badminton and those boring giggling parties. What I've got. . .you couldn't begin to understand!'

What can you say to something like that? I stood gawping at her, as if I really did have a gap where my front teeth ought to be.

'So no foursomes, Jo. And. . .I'm sorry but I don't want you to meet Paolo, or anything like that. I just don't want him thinking I'm a silly schoolgirl who has to bring all my mates in on the act.'

'Why not? Is he married or something?' I stormed. I'd kept quiet long enough and my anger had made me say the first nasty thing that came into my head.

'He's twenty-one, he's a creative director of Toppers hairdressing salon, he drives a white Cortina estate and lives in a three-room flat near the park. Alone. No, he's not married. Never has been. Is there anything else you'd like to know?' Kim said coldly.

'Kim. . .I'm sorry. Honest. But you have to admit that it's going to sound a bit. . .well a bit sudden to me. I've been away five weeks, and all this has happened, and I don't even know the guy, and I don't know what to say. . .' I stammered, blushing, scraping at the pavement with the toe of my scuffed shoe.

'Say nothing, then. I really don't need your advice any more, Jo,' Kim murmured, shaking her streaky-blonde hair. And then she turned and walked off up the school drive without looking back.

I ran to catch up with her, trying to reach through the barriers she was putting up.

'Anyway, Kim, I'm happy for you. I really am. You

deserve something good. I'm glad it's good! And what d'you reckon about me and Tony?' I panted.

'Great.' she said, without much emotion. 'But you'll probably outgrow him, won't you?'

'I don't think so. . .' I muttered, deflated.

Marie waved madly at me from the top of the school drive, and came careering down, like a red-haired runaway tyre.

'Hi, Jo. . .Kim. . .Mandy's having a big party, end of the month. Fancy dress! Great idea, eh? C'mon. We're all going. It's one of those parties where you have to dress up as tramps, and if the weather holds we're going to have a barbecue in the back garden. Tony'll be able to come, too, won't he Jo? And. . .what about your new fella, Kim?' she grinned.

I shook my head at her behind Kim's back. Kim just smiled.

'I don't think so,' she said, walking away again.

'Huh! What did I tell you? If you ask me, whatever she's got, I don't want it. Hope it's not catching,' Marie snorted.

'It's love,' I said.

'That's what she calls it?'

'She'll be OK, once she gets used to the idea and settles down. She's just gone a bit uppity for the moment,' I said.

'Maybe you're right. You know her better than any of us. I *hope* you're right, for all our sakes! What've you found out about this Italian, anyway?' Marie asked.

'Not a lot. Wish I could suss him out,' I murmured.

Marie nudged me, with a wicked smile creasing the corners of her wide mouth.

'Isn't it time you got your hair done?' she asked.

'Well. . .that's an idea!' I whispered.

Chapter 3

I had to be crazy. That was the only explanation for it. But egged on by your mates, you'll do anything. And in the background, at the back of my mind, there was Tony, who'd told me on the phone to leave well alone, when I told him about Kim.

'Remember Barbie?' he'd asked. 'The shy dark-haired girl with the glasses? She went through that a few months back, got herself involved with this idiot who played the saxophone in the band at one of the hotels. Wouldn't speak to anyone. Treated us all as if we were bad smells. And then, a few weeks later, it was all over, and she was back as if nothing'd happened. You'll see. Kim'll come round in her own good time.'

It was sensible advice, and I'd always taken his advice in the past. But I reckoned that this time he didn't quite realize how worried I was. I just wanted to set my mind at rest, that was all. Marie agreed with me when we went swimming on Monday night.

In fact, she'd come to the phone-box with me on Tuesday lunchtime, and looked up the phone number of Toppers for me, and stood over me and tried not to giggle as I made the appointment for Wednesday, half-past four.

Now, I was starting to change my mind again, standing across the road from Toppers, wondering if trembly knees and confusion was the price I had to pay for nosiness.

Because that was at the back of it all, no matter how I'd tried to tell myself that I was Kim's keeper. I was just plainly and simply curious about this guy who could take over my best friend so completely that she'd hardly give me the time of day.

Even Mum hadn't believed me when I'd told her I was going to have my hair sorted out. She'd looked at me and then a slow sly grin had come over her face and she'd said, 'I see. . .'. The trouble with Mum was that she was all ears when I was on the phone to anyone. She'd heard me talking about Kim to Tony. And even she'd seen through my awkward pretence at concern over my hair. So what?

I crossed the road quickly, before I could chicken out of the whole thing, and pushed open the door of the hairdressing salon.

'Miss Farmer, half-past four,' I stammered to the girl in reception, without taking a breath.

'Oh yesss. . .' she hissed, affectedly. 'With Mr Paolo, isn't it?'

I nodded, and she gave me the up and down glance, silent but effective.

I knew I was a mess, but here, in the dark red

salon entrance, surrounded by gleaming chrome and shimmery glass, and stacks of glossy magazines, I felt like an escaped haystack. Not only that, I was still in my school uniform.

The girl on reception must've been about my age, sixteen or seventeen, and she was in a kind of uniform, too, a high-necked cossack shirt in a cranberry colour, and a straight black button-through skirt. But she was sleek enough, and made-up enough to have just stepped out of a UFO. My grey uniform skirt hem was unravelling, I'd caught it on a desk in the computer room that morning. And there was a darker grey stain on my pale grey polo-neck where some mayonnaise from my packed-lunch salad sandwiches had squeezed out at lunchtime and dropped in a big yellow blob. Then there was the smudge of ink just by the side of my nose. And my hair! Did I really have to think about my hair?

'Would you follow me, please?' another space-age assistant murmured in my left ear as she flung a silvery overall round me.

Hairdressing salons had never been like this in the days when Mum took me to Renée's on the corner of our street to have my fringe cut into a one-inch pelmet. Renée's had put me off hairdressers completely by the age of eleven, and since then, I'd chopped at my unruly curls myself. Catching sight of myself in the cruel mirrors that lined every wall made me cringe with embarrassment.

Inside, the place was more chrome chairs and shiny red plastic. The assistants floated like oiled robots in those red blouses, with silvery metallic trousers and silvery eyelids and red plastic lips to match. How could Kim have talked herself into coming in here? It terrified me more than the dentist's.

The assistant pulled out a chair for me, plonked me down with a gentle pressure from her red-nailed hand, and told me that Mr Paolo would be with me shortly. A girl in the next chair with kitchen foil wrapped round her head like a swimming cap leaned over to me.

'What colour are you going?' she murmured.

Pale! I nearly said.

'Dunno,' I muttered.

'I was fuschia last month, just on the tips, but I'm going back to natural. Natural's in, you know! Trouble is, I can't remember what my natural is! Who's doing yours?' she asked.

'Mr Paolo.'

'Ooh, nice! He's the best. Don't worry about a thing. If he says two inches all over, just agree. He knows what he's doing,' she smiled, reassuringly.

I wasn't reassured at all. I wanted to go, now, before ET and his little mates started crawling up out of the plugholes in the back-washes. Two inches all over! With my nose? Even Tony would never forgive me for that.

'Hi!' a guy's voice smiled from behind me.

I blinked, and looked into the mirror. The famous Paolo! I blinked again. Surely not?

He wasn't the least like the person I'd expected. In my mind's eye he'd been short and smoulderingly dark and slimy, like a well-fed slug on legs, probably with platform shoes, a white shirt open to the bottom button, a wide leather belt and tight trousers on his stumpy legs.

This guy, smiling at me through the mirror, fluffing my hair about expertly with his hands, was a human being, a tall slim human being in an oversized blue sweater with the sleeves pushed up, and jeans, and the most amazing twinkle in his soft brown eyes.

He stopped fluffing up my hair, leaned over my shoulder, and asked my reflection in the mirror,

'What're you doing here?'

I'd been sussed! How? Through my name in the appointments book? Through my school uniform? Through Kim's deadly accurate description of her nosy best friend who might come snooping around? But my name in the appointments book wasn't Joanne, but 'Miss Farmer', and my school uniform was covered by the silver sheet, and why should Kim describe me to him?

'What. . .what're you on about?' I stammered, trying to cover up.

'This hair. It doesn't need any work on it. It's fantastic, thick. . .and this natural wave. Masses of it. You know, some women spend a fortune on soft perms, and years growing their hair to this length and this condition! And the colour! Chestnut. Great! What've you been putting on it? Henna?' he asked.

I nodded, goggle-eyed. Tony always raved about my thick unmanageable hair, but I'd sort of taken it for granted. 'Henna. Yeah. My. . .' I was going to say that my boyfriend suggested I used it, which was true, but for some reason I didn't. For some reason.

'That explains the condition, and the colour.

Well. . .let's see. Nothing much I can do to improve the look. Gemma, just a wash, no conditioner, and I'll trim a bit more shape into the front, so that it just lifts from your face. OK?' he smiled.

'OK,' I agreed, breathing again.

Gemma washed my hair and swathed it in a towel, and led me back to Paolo. The experience was turning out much better than I'd expected. Except for one thing. Guilt was gnawing away at my insides as his scissors clipped tiny wet strands from my hair. I had to say something.

'I. . .I think you. . .er. . .know my mate, Kim,' I muttered.

'Kim?' he asked, smiling widely. 'You're a friend of hers?'

'Yeah. And I'd sort of like to ask you a favour. . . Don't tell her I came. Please don't mention it. I was wrong to nose. You see, I've been away on holiday, and when I came back she was raving about this boyfriend, and she's gone right off, none of us can talk to her, so I thought it had to be your fault, and I came here to look you over. Sounds awful when I say it right out like that, doesn't it? It feels awful, now, too. You know, as if I'm spying on her. . .'

'You must be Joanne!' he said. I couldn't tell what he meant by that, or whether he approved or disapproved, because he was bending down plugging the hair-drier in, and I couldn't see his face.

'That's me. Joanne. The famous idiot who won't keep out of her mate's private life!' I said, with a wrinkly frown, trying to apologize.

Paolo turned the drier on, and started to fluff my

hair dry. He looked worried. I felt even more of an interfering old cow than ever.

'You're her best friend, aren't you?' he murmured, quietly.

'I *was*,' I groaned.

'I'm glad you came. Kim's dead set against my meeting you for some reason', he said. 'I'd like to talk to you.' He glanced at his watch. 'Look, I've got Mrs Simms to blow dry, and then I'm finished. If I let Gemma finish you, I can get on with Mrs Simms, and we could have a coffee. There's things I want to ask you about. . .but not here. Not at work. . .'

'Er. . . Kim doesn't know I'm here. . .' I muttered.

'And you don't want her to know, and you don't want to bump into her, or anyone else while you're with me. I understand. I knew you'd be a thoughtful sort of person, from what Kim's said about you. Three doors along from here there's Dino's restaurant. He doesn't open till seven, but he'll always make me a coffee. I've never taken Kim there, and he's a friend of mine. So? Tap on the door. He'll let you in.'

He smiled, that wide friendly smile, putting me immediately at my ease. There was no difficulty, either, in getting him to see my problem, or in finding a solution, immediately. That felt odd. With most of the boys I knew, even with Tony, often, there were long involved explanations and endless discussions about what to do. No one ever seemed to want to make a decision. Not like this guy.

'Right,' I said.

In ten minutes I was dried and sparkling. I looked

29

good. The untamed look of my hair hadn't been ruined, but sort of stylized. I felt good. I felt even better when I tapped on Dino's restaurant window, and Paolo himself let me in, and led me to a dim table in the corner.

How the other half live, it was. I'd been to the Chinese a few times with our crowd and to the Wimpy and McDonald's and Hamburger Heaven, but except for that time my brother, Roy, had come home on a visit from Australia, I'd never been to a proper restaurant.

Even at half-past five in the afternoon, it looked beautiful. The tables had been set with pink cloths and napkins in tall shimmery glasses, and there was a bowl of pale carnations on each table, with a pink candle, in a holder, in the centre of each bowl. They weren't the grubby whitish worn-down candles in bottles that were on the tables in the folk club in Brighton. They were all fresh and new, pretty as the flowers at their base. All the seats were pink dralon. I felt out of place, squeezing into the corner settee with Paolo.

'Glad you could make it,' he said, as if I were doing him a big favour. Then this waiter, with a cloth over his arm, put down a silver tray in front of us, and unloaded pink silver-banded cups and elegant silver pots, one of coffee, one of milk, and a plate of marzipan biscuit things. I couldn't pour. My fingernails were too grubby for public inspection in a place like that. I sat on my hands. But I needn't've bothered. The waiter poured both coffees, and then disappeared, like a ghost.

I was dead impressed. And just a bit out of my depth. But Paolo looked right at home. He'd slipped a leather jacket over his sweater. It looked as expensive as the place we were in.

'Kim. . .' he murmured.

I'd almost forgotten why we were there.

'Oh, yes. Kim. . .' I said, wishing I could get rid of that ink-smudge between my fingers.

'Kim's got problems. She's a very sad little girl,' Paolo said, gently. 'I like her. I'm very fond of her. I think she means a great deal to both of us, doesn't she, Joanne?'

'Yeah. Sure,' I agreed.

'Let me tell you about it. . .' he said quietly.

The way he told it wasn't the way Kim had told it, not at all. The way Paolo told it, I could understand. I could feel it all happening. He was taking me into his confidence, as a friend, Kim's best friend. And there was no phoniness in what he said. He made that clear from the start.

'I knew Carl,' he said. 'Kim's brother. Years ago. We were here at college together for a year and then I went off to London. I arrived back, in this new job, wanting to look up old friends, and I looked Carl up. I didn't know. . .'

I froze inside. Carl's death, in that motorbike accident had been front-page news in our city. But it had been a nightmare for Kim, one she'd only recently started to wake from. She worshipped Carl.

'I knocked on his door out of the blue. I said "Is Carl in?" and this girl, this blushing girl who'd opened the door, started to cry. I said "He's not in?

31

He's. . ." And she said, "He died. Last August!" I never knew. And I never knew he had a sister. Not such a sister as Kim, so. . . I don't know. . . so open, so easily touched, so sad. You understand?'

I nodded. That's how Kim had always seemed to me. Until recently.

'I didn't know what to do. This girl's crying, she's alone in the house. I wanted to help her. I listened. She told me about Carl, brought photographs.'

I sighed. I'd had all that. The photographs. The tears. It was something Marie and Ellen and the others had never seen. They'd only known the moodiness.

'And I said, "Come out with me. I'm lonely, too." You see, that's the way to help. But you know that, Joanne, don't you? She told me about you. But. . . it's all wrong.'

'What's wrong?' I asked.

'Kim. She's. . . not understanding. She doesn't know that I wanted just to help, when her best friend was on holiday. She's. . .'

'She's fallen in love with you,' I helped him out.

'And how do I tell her, I'm just a friend? I've styled her hair. I've taken her to the seaside. I've tried to give her confidence. But what do I do now, Joanne? She's so possessive. She needs me all to herself, and that's not what I wanted.'

'What did you want?' I asked.

'I don't know. I honestly don't know,' he muttered, his brown eyes were troubled. 'We're her friends, aren't we? Would you want to be in my place, to tell her not to fall in love?'

'No,' I admitted.

'But, you'll help? I need a friend, too. I need some help with this one. I have to be gentle!'

'Right,' I agreed.

'So. . . tomorrow night, I'll see her. I'll try to tell her this. You look after her, Joanne. You'll see her each day. Be sure she's all right? I'll be as careful as I can.'

'Good,' I murmured.

'And. . . if I could meet you again. Saturday? I'll see if it works. You could meet me on Saturday? Nine o'clock. In the car-park by the river path? Tell me, then, if Kim's all right.'

I didn't stop, even to think. I was just drowning in the look in his eyes.

'OK. I'll meet you,' I agreed.

'Joanne. I've needed a friend like you,' he said, touching my hand on the pink tablecloth.

I wouldn't like to say what I felt, at that moment.

Chapter 4

Disaster struck, right the next morning. I wasn't in any mood for disasters, either. I'd spent the night wondering how I was going to help Kim through it when Paolo finally told her that she'd read more into his friendship than was really there. I'd done a lot of thinking about how the whole thing had built up in her mind, out of all proportion, and I stopped feeling angry about the way she'd been treating me. I could understand how someone like Paolo, so different from any of the gawky useless boys I knew could make her fall so heavily.

Kim was a bit more approachable that morning, and although she was still doing her looking-down-the-nose act, we actually managed an almost normal conversation on the bus. Or was that because I was trying, just that bit harder, to take it gently with her?

Anyway, the disaster was called Marie. She came hurtling down the road at us both, dragging a misera-ble-looking Mandy behind her.

'You two aren't going to let Mandy down, are you?' she demanded elbowing her way between Kim and me. 'You've heard? The party's had to be put forward to this Saturday, because her mum and dad've been invited to a big posh do on the Saturday she'd arranged. It's awful. Nikki and Jim cried off, and Angie's going to London at the weekend with the rest of the basketball team, and that leaves only about ten people who're dead certs to come. But I told Mandy she could count on you two. She can, can't she?'

She didn't even mention my hair, or blurt out, tactlessly about my meeting with Paolo. This crisis about Mandy's party had knocked everything else out of her fizzy head. But Saturday, I was supposed to be meeting Paolo. . .

'I think you can count me out,' Kim sniffed. 'I don't know what plans Paolo's made for the weekend, but he did mention that he might take me out for a meal, somewhere.'

'Aw c'mon, Kim. Don't be such a wet blanket. Find a bit of room for Mandy's party. It'll be no good if we can't make people come! We can count on you, though, can't we, Joanne!' she smiled, tucking her arm through mine. 'Tony's not around yet, so there's no one to take you out to dinner!' she sneered gently at Kim. 'And Jack and Sam from badminton're still coming, so we need you as spare girl to keep spotty Sam talking while we all grab Jack! OK?'

I wobbled a smile at her.

'Saturday?' I stammered. Saturday, Kim wouldn't be going out to dinner with Paolo. On Saturday, I'd be meeting him in the car-park, to tell him how Kim was taking the news that he was only a friend. . . 'Saturday. I dunno. I don't know if my gran's coming round. . .'

'Please, Joanne!' Mandy wailed.

'You're coming. Give your gran a pile of boogy records, and leave her to amuse herself. We need you, Jo. Half-past seven. At Mandy's!' Marie smiled. She wasn't to be argued with. And then, still dragging poor old Mandy, she raced off to collar Ellen, who was just getting off her moped at the school gates.

And that was it. I couldn't really wriggle out of it. I was going to have to think of a better excuse than Gran. I *had* to make the meeting with Paolo.

But by the next morning, I still hadn't come up with anything. And then, there was Kim.

I knew by her face, that Friday, that Paolo had

told her it was off. She'd forgotten the blue eye-liner. Or perhaps she'd cried away the make-up on her way to our house. She certainly looked upset. I just didn't know what to say or do. Paolo had asked me to keep an eye on her, but how did I open the subject of what was wrong with her?

'Jo,' she muttered, as we stood in this terrible aching silence at the bus-stop, 'I. . .er. . . I happen to be free tomorrow. So I thought I'd do Mandy a favour, and go to her party. I'll call for you at quarter-past seven, if you like.'

It was a breakthrough. It was what I'd been waiting for. And yet, it was at the wrong time, completely the wrong time. How could I be at the party with Kim, listening to her problems, and seeing Paolo, and reassuring him at the same time?

It was the old old problem of Joanne the mother hen, who clucked around poking her beak into so many problems that she started falling over her own spindly legs.

'OK. That'll be great,' I murmured.

And it had to be. I'd let too many people down if I didn't turn up at the party. There was only one way out of the mess. I was going to have to get a badly upset stomach at the party, at exactly half past eight. That would just give me time to race round to the car park to meet Paolo at nine.

It wasn't really in my line. I'd never had to have secrets, and never gone in for lies and deception, and I didn't much like the person I was having to be.

'Just this once. Never again!' I told myself, as I made up very carefully on Saturday night.

It wasn't worth it. In fact, this made-up story about the stomach upset wasn't going to be as phoney as I'd imagined. Already my stomach was churning over and over with panic.

And the funny thing was that I didn't once stop to wonder if I could cancel the meeting with Paolo. The thought never crossed my mind. For some reason, I dressed with him in mind, pulling on a silky blue dress that skimmed my shape and flicking out my hair into a chestnut cloud.

I forgot about the fancy-dress you see. And I only remembered when I saw Kim standing on the door-step in a pair of her dad's old trousers and a huge patched jacket and battered straw hat.

'Aren't you dressing up?' she stammered, all nervously. 'I thought everyone had to! Aw, Joanne, I can't go like this, not with you dressed normally. What if no one else is in fancy dress – I'll feel an idiot!'

Just like the old Kim. That flashy confidence had gone for a moment. My stomach churned more angrily as I looked at her, and saw the scared expression in her eyes. I leaned on the door-frame.

'It's just that. . . I'm not feeling very well, Kim. Don't know how long I can last out. I reckon I'm coming down with a bug, so I've just pulled this dress on, 'cos it's the easiest thing I've got. I'm feeling really queasy!'

'You look it, actually,' Kim murmured, squeezing my arm. 'D'you want to call if off? We could just sit round here and play records or something. Mandy's'll be a bit childish for me.'

'And let Mandy down?' I sighed. Liar. The part was killing me. It was wrong. It was all wrong. Just when things looked to be coming out right, too.

But I'd convinced Kim, and in a way that hurt, too, to be handing out lies when she was trying to cope with a truth that had been hard to swallow.

'Paolo's gone away this weekend. To London, I think. He said he might ring me on Sunday when he gets back,' she told me, on the way to Mandy's.

'Oh yeah?' I asked, feeling even more like a heel than ever. 'Still the big thing, is it?' I was fishing.

'It's. . .' she started to say, and then Sam and Jack, and Lee and Ellen yelled from behind us, and came clattering up to join us.

They looked fantastic. Ellen had even smudged her face all over, and Lee had blackened his front teeth. Jack had an enormous pair of boots on, over his trainers, with no laces, so they banged about, and he had to drag his feet along to keep them on.

'First time I've seen a tramp in makeup, wearing a posh frock,' Ellen murmured, looking me over.

'She's not feeling well,' Kim said, quickly.

'Well enough to freak out your hair, and put lipstick on, though?' Ellen grinned. 'Who're you trying to impress, Jo? Watch out Sam! This could be your lucky night!'

Sam blushed. Not half as deeply as I did. Trust Ellen to put her big sarky foot in it! I thought I'd better play it her way.

'I'm counting on you to catch me if I pass out!' I winked at Sam, hoping that it looked as if I was being very brave, despite feeling rotten.

'Don't encourage him, Jo! He looks dead shy, but there's no telling what he might do with a bit of pushing,' Lee teased.

They were always getting at Sam. It took the pressure off me this time, and everyone was laughing when we arrived at Mandy's.

The place was packed. The basketball match had been called off, and there were friends of friends who'd arrived to boost up the numbers. The amplifiers from the music centre had been trailed into the garden and were booming out disco hits. About twenty tramps were trying to dance on the patio, and thirty or forty more were gathered round this huge barbecue that Mandy's dad had made. It was really rocking.

I hardly recognized anyone. They were all hidden under layers of old clothes, but the tramp who came over with some glasses of punch for us was definitely Mandy, in a fantastic old tail coat and lop-sided bow-tie. She raised her eyebrows at me.

'Sorry Mandy,' I muttered. 'I feel awful. But I thought I'd better call round in case we all had to pretend to be six people. I might have to dash off home, soon.'

'You never said you felt as ill as that!' Kim frowned. 'Is it that bad?'

''Fraid so. I'll just sit down for a minute or two,' I muttered, making for the cast-iron bench at the edge of the patio.

I felt rotten, and not with stomach upset, either. The party looked as if it was going to be the best for ages, and I was going to miss it. Mandy's dad had strung fairy lights in the trees and there were big trestle tables on the lawn all laid out with salads and bread and brightly-coloured plates.

'Joanne. . . let me take you back,' Kim begged me, perching on the edge of the bench next to me.

But just at that moment, Jack came along, and swung her off to dance, leaving Sam looking hopefully at me.

'I have to go. Sorry Sam. . .' I said.

I found Mandy, and muttered more apologies, and weaved through the crowds to Kim, who was dancing awkwardly, with Jack.

'Look after my mate, Jack!' I yelled over the music.

'I'm coming. . .' Kim argued.

'No. It's OK. Honest. Stay,' I told her, pointing her back towards the dancing.

She looked a bit lost, but I knew that Jack would see she was OK. That was one thing off my conscience. As soon as I got to the corner of Orchard Avenue, and out of sight of Mandy's house, I started running.

It was quarter to nine. What if Paolo wouldn't wait for me? But he would. He'd gone to all that trouble to make sure Kim didn't find out we were meeting to talk about her, even telling her that he was going to London for the weekend. He was pretty thoughtful, and obviously fond enough of her to want to protect her.

Would Tony do the same for me?

I stopped running. The entrance to the car park was ahead of me, and there was time, five minutes at least, to settle myself down before meeting Paolo.

But that sudden flash of thought about Tony surprised me. I hadn't really thought about him for days.

That picture I'd been holding on to, in my memory, the one of Tony and me on the beach at Brighton, had faded already. At night, in bed, all I'd thought about was Kim, and her problems.

And Paolo.

I'd thought about Paolo a lot. I'd remembered those very dark eyes, that quiet confidence that had put me immediately at ease, the tenderness in his voice when he spoke about Kim.

And the touch of his hand.

I remembered that, too, with a sharpness that edged the memory in bright light, and hurt. Because every time I remembered, I wanted to pull my hand back in delayed shock. Nothing had ever made me feel like that before, not Tony's smile, not Tony's gentle squeezing of my hand, not Tony's kisses. Nothing, ever, had turned me upside down like that touch.

It was the touch that had made me a liar. I'd been lying even to myself. Did I want to go through with it?

'Joanne!' Paolo called to me from across the car-park.

I hesitated for just a split second. Then I ran towards him.

Chapter 5

'How's Kim?' Paolo asked as soon as he'd settled me in the car.

'Very quiet. A bit like her old self. I s'pose you told her. . .' I said.

He looked thoughtful, and then started the car up.

'It's a slow job. It's got to be. I just said I wouldn't see her this weekend. I told her to go out and see her friends. Is that what she's doing?' he asked.

The car swung out of the car-park. I didn't ask where we were going. I didn't think to. But the sensible down-to-earth way he was talking to me settled all the crazy ideas that had been flashing round in my mind. He was making it clear that we were talking about Kim, and that we were only meeting for Kim's sake. Fair enough. I'd been losing sight of that.

'She's at a party,' I muttered.

He glanced briefly in my direction.

'What kind of party?' he asked.

'Oh, you know the sort of thing – all dressed up as tramps, fruit punch, fairy lights in the trees, and mum and dad cooking hamburgers,' I said airily.

'Not your kind of thing?' he asked. 'Eh, Joanne?'

I laughed.

'No! Not my kind of thing!' I lied.

'Now, let me guess. Let me guess what you like. . . Quiet. . . water. . . yes. . . you look the kind of girl who loves riversides, the sea. . .'

'The sea! Yeah!' I agreed.

'Brighton?'

''Course. You knew. Kim told you,' I smiled.

'And this boyfriend of yours, he's in Brighton,' Paolo said, turning off the by-pass into the road to North Alton.

'Tony. He's an art student,' I said. And even saying Tony's name didn't screw me up too tightly. It wasn't that kind of conversation. He was very easy to talk to.

'Student? Hmm. He paints your portrait?' Paolo asked.

I shook my head.

'He paints *things*, you know. . . buildings, landscapes, stuff like that,' I said.

'A pity to ignore you, though!' Paolo smiled.

'I've never thought of it like that,' I agreed.

'I'd paint you, Joanne,' Paolo murmured. And then he smiled, broadly, as if to say that it was just a friendly compliment, nothing to worry about.

But I wasn't worried. I watched the dusky hedgerows speed past the windows of the car, and the moon caught in the trees. I thought of Mandy's party and the noise, and spotty Sam, and the kids all crowding round Mandy's dad giving him expert instruction on how to cook sausages. Paolo could be right. Quiet was what I liked. This kind of quiet.

'Kim's. . . Kim's much better tonight,' I said, breaking the silence.

'Oh. . . Kim. . . Yes. Good. Sorry, Joanne. I was thinking,' Paolo said absent-mindedly. 'I was thinking about someone else, just for the moment and. . . Look. There's a pub. Come in, I'll buy you a drink, and we can talk about Kim and me. . . and you.'

'I'm. . . I'm not really supposed to go in pubs,' I stammered awkwardly.

Paolo banged the steering wheel with the palms of his hands, and laughed.

'Sorry! I forgot! How old are you. . . seventeen?'

'Sixteen,' I said in a small voice.

'You see, with Kim, there's no problem. I think of her as a kid sister, around fourteen. It's coffee for Kim. But she's the same age as you, isn't she? I find that hard to believe. Honestly!'

He turned to look at me. And then his expression changed. He stared, as if he was looking at me for the very first time, intently, half-dazed. I couldn't swallow. My mouth was getting all dry. . .

'We'll have a steak sandwich then, in the restaurant. That's allowed, isn't it?' he said, as if snapping out of a trance.

'Yes,' I croaked.

I had problems getting out of the car. My legs had turned to jelly. And the night that had looked so warm and scented from the inside of the car, was unexpectedly cold. I shivered. Paolo wrapped my cardigan round my shoulders for me, and his hand brushed my cheek accidentally.

The suddenness of the movement caught me off guard. I turned to say something to him, but I couldn't. He was too close. It almost scared me.

'Come on,' he said, taking my hand.

Did I finally stop pretending then, at that moment, that I was doing all this for Kim? Or had I only been pretending to myself, all along? However it was, from then on the conversation started to get a bit awkward. There were too many unexplained sparks flying.

I tried to remember, as I sat at the window table of the pub, looking out over the river, if I'd ever felt this way about Tony. I couldn't make the connection. Because it was all so different.

I thought of that first day of school, with Kim, when she'd seemed so phoney and so superior, going on about the grubby Leisure Centre, and the kids' stuff. But I was starting to get that feeling, now.

There was a stillness about this pub on the river that there'd never much been in any of the places I'd gone to with Tony. The cafés in Brighton were always crowded with mates and loud chatter. There'd been the walks. . . but nothing like this. . . I looked over my shoulder towards the bar, where Paolo was ordering my coke. I'd felt an idiot ordering that. I felt a bit of an idiot being here, in a way, just a little out of place. It was the first time I'd been in a pub, even though this was the restaurant section. Inside, it was all rosy light and panelled walls with the sort of hunting prints that Tony would've turned his nose up at. But they looked OK to me. And outside, there were floodlights on the silver river and the silhouettes of distant trees. No one was shouting or screeching with laughter. There weren't any pinball machines or plastic cups. I could grow to like this. . .

And Paolo.

I liked his smile. It wasn't wobbly and uneven like Tony's. It was a smile that said, right out, that the guy behind it was pretty certain about what made him happy.

I liked the way he dressed, casual, but smartish: leather jacket, soft sweaters, pressed jeans with a real crease down the front.

I liked his hair, a soft dark brown thick flop, curling softly just at the level of his ear-lobes.

I liked being with him. That was the crunch. I actually liked being here, with him, away from the grot and the racket and the sarky jokes.

'What's on your mind?' he whispered, coming up behind me silently, and putting my drink and my steak sandwich down in front of me.

I shrugged.

'Tony?' he asked.

'How. . . how did you guess?' I breathed.

'The far-away look. It's the look I get when I remember Elizabeth,' he grinned. 'My childhood sweetheart. Sat in front of me in class. Used to pass sweets to me, behind her chair. I was madly in love with her when I was seven. And I stayed in love with her, just a little in love with her, right until the time she left school and moved with her parents to the North. I was heartbroken.'

'How long did it last?' I asked.

'Oh. . . at least six months!' he laughed.

I bit into my steak sandwich, hoping the butter wouldn't squodge everywhere and show me up.

'Mind you, some childhood romances do last,' Paolo added. 'How long's it been with Tony?'

'Six years,' I said, swallowing.

'A pity. . .' he murmured.

'What is?'

'Oh, nothing. Just a pity you're so committed, that's all. . .' he whispered.

'Why?' I breathed.

'Because. . . you know very well why, Joanne! You're reading me just as clearly as I'm reading you, aren't you? Isn't that the problem between us? Wasn't it always the problem right from the first? D'you want to talk about Kim?'

I shook my head, slowly.

'Me, neither. But both of us want to make sure Kim's OK? And what about Tony?' he asked, gently.

'I. . . I don't know,' I murmured.

Then, without a signal, we were both standing up and walking out together. We'd neither of us said exactly how we felt. He just understood. That was the amazing thing. He knew exactly what was happening, almost as if he could see into my mind.

He settled me into the car, and drove away, fast. The clock on the dashboard read twenty past ten. I'd told Mum I'd be home by eleven. I just hoped we'd make it.

We didn't say a word on the way back. He drove. I looked out of the window, and said nothing, just wondered if I was ready to take on the risk of loving him. And then I directed him to our estate. As we passed the end of Orchard Avenue there was just a flicker of coloured lights in the end garden, where I should have been. Paolo pulled the car in by the park gates.

'I'll see you on Wednesday,' he said.

'I. . . I dunno. . .' I muttered. There was Kim to

think of. And Tony. And the mess I was making of my feelings.

He leaned forward, took my face in his hands and pulled me towards him. I felt as if I were melting, right down to my toes, as his kiss trembled first against my lips, and then reached right inside me.

I'd never been kissed into a daze before.

'Don't worry. We'll just have to be careful with Kim and Tony. We'll let them go slowly. It's going to be all right. We can't give this up, Jo. I've never felt this close to anyone before,' he whispered, twining his fingers in my hair.

'Me neither,' I said, hoarsely.

'Until Wednesday. Car-park. Eight?' he asked.

'Wednesday,' I said, letting myself out of the car.

I hardly slept that night. My head throbbed with guilt and a sizzling electric buzz. Perhaps I hadn't known what love was all about before. It had always seemed soft, like clouds, like cotton wool, like the warmth of sunshine and summer days. This love was like thunderstorms, all lightning brightness and dark heaviness between the forks of memory. It made me feel sick, and ill, and yet it felt necessary.

Kim called the next morning. I was still hazy, still not too steady on my legs, still shaking after that kiss.

'Called to see how you are,' she said, but there wasn't any of the nervous friendliness in her voice that I'd heard the night before. 'You look terrible.'

'Yeah. . . sorry I missed the party,' I mumbled.

'You didn't miss anything worth missing,' she said, wearily, flicking through my records. 'It was the usual. Jack got off with Angie, and Sam went home in a huff. Lee went round telling everyone how many sausages he'd eaten, Sue Fraser's got a new boyfriend. That's the news. Pathetic, isn't it? I left at ten. I thought Paolo just might phone me from London.'

'He didn't?' I asked, anxiously.

'No. He rang this morning. He's coming round for me at seven tonight. After last night, I can't wait to see him again. He's got the right idea y'know. Who needs kids' parties and dressing up as tramps? I don't,' she said triumphantly.

Suddenly, I wanted to blow that smile off her face. It would only take one stinging reference to last night. I wanted to tell her that she had no right to come in, lording it over me, when I was the one Paolo wanted to be with, and she was on the way out.

'The party was OK,' I sniffed, covering up.

'Maybe for you, Jo,' she said, snottily. 'But not for me. Not any more. . . Anyway, got to rush. Paolo likes me to look good, so it'll take me a while to get ready.'

She needed to be brought down with a huge crash for speaking to me as if I was something that had just crawled out blindly from under a stone.

But then, I thought, Paolo probably wanted to see her tonight to finish with her. Of course. And although she was riding high today, she'd be devastated by tomorrow. It always hurts more when you've been bragging about it, the way she had.

The jealousy gave way to a tide of pity for my old mate who was heading straight towards heartbreak.

'Take care, Kim,' I said quietly.

She laughed.

'Don't be stupid! Think I don't know what I'm doing? Trouble with you is that you've been smothering me, Joanne, with your so-called sympathy. You don't like it now that I'm happy, do you? You're like all the others. Everyone's jealous of me!' she smirked. 'See you, Jo. Hope your stomach upset clears up for school. I'll call round tomorrow, anyway!'

She waved her fingers at me, confidently, before she flounced out. I buried my face in my hands, and cried. And I didn't know whether I was crying for Kim, or for Paolo, or for Tony, or for me. Me, probably. And why not?

Chapter 6

Everyone was full of the party, and what everybody'd done and said in non-stop boring detail. It was always like that. The whole week was taken up with what had happened on Saturday, until Friday morning when they all started talking about what they hoped would happen on the coming Saturday night.

I walked through the playground, sat in the classroom, marched between lessons, in a tight painful dreamworld, listening to snippets of conversation.

'No, honest, I *never* thought I'd get off with him. . .'

'So why did you hang on to him from the moment he walked in then?'

'Y'know what that bitchy Sue Fraser said to me?'

'Didn't Marie show herself up, slobbering all over the boy from the record shop? I was embarrassed for her!'

'That's only 'cos you fancied him yourself!'

On and on it went. Anyone would think that the most important thing in the whole world was the state of everyone's personal romance.

I'd never really been a part of that, not while I had my long-standing childhood romance to keep me going. But until now I'd always enjoyed the after-party action replays, the bitchiness and the starry eyes. Now it didn't mean a thing.

What I wanted to know, and what I couldn't find out, was what had happened between Kim and Paolo. Kim was like a closed book. On Monday morning she was back into her big superior act, and I couldn't make out whether that was a cover-up for the end of the romance, or whether Paolo had felt as achingly sorry for her as I had, and hadn't been able to come right out and tell her that he was packing her in.

'So what happened to you on Saturday night?' Marie burbled, button-holing me on Monday lunch-time. 'You missed my big scene with Gary from the record shop. He's crazy about me, Jo. You only had to look at him to see that! I couldn't get rid of him. . . I wish you'd seen it.'

'Hope he lasts longer than Norm from Benidorm.

You'll get yourself a reputation as a one-date wonder, Marie, if you go on like that!' I snapped.

Marie looked as if she'd been slapped. The big chubby smile on her face sagged.

'What's up with you? I thought it was a stomach upset you had. Sounds more like a heart upset to me. Something wrong between you and Tony?' Ellen chipped in, coming to Marie's defence.

'Nothing at all. It's just that I'm having problems keeping up with all these on-off romances, and the fuss everyone makes of them. Isn't it time some of you settled down a bit?'

'Oh, listen to High and Mighty! You sound just like Kim Saunders. She's a pain, too!' Ellen hissed at me.

'Ellen. . .it's OK. . .Maybe you're still not feeling very well, eh, Jo?' Marie asked, nervously.

I was really sorry I'd snapped. I didn't want to hurt Marie. She was harmless, just a plump cheerful girl who lived and breathed for falling in love. I'd never heard her say a bad word about anyone.

'Sorry, Marie. I reckon I'm not myself today,' I muttered.

'Coming swimming tonight?' she asked, brightening.

'Better not,' I said. 'Still a bit queasy.'

'Oh yeah. Right,' she grinned.

I breathed a sigh of relief. I wished everyone was as easy to get on with as Marie. But Ellen was still looking at me suspiciously and coldly.

I'd definitely got on the wrong side of her. Part of me worried about that. I didn't want to make an enemy of Ellen. As a mate she was good, but I knew that if I got at Marie again, she'd have a real go at me, just as I'd've done, in the old days, for Kim. But at the moment Kim was really getting on my nerves.

Tony rang on Monday night. I'd almost forgotten about his regular phone calls and how much I'd looked forward to the sound of his voice. Usually, no matter how upset I was, or how fed up with school and my mates, talking to Tony on the phone put me back in touch with my own natural cheerfulness.

But the phone call got off to a bad start. Tony started telling me about what had happened at the folk club on Saturday night, and how they'd all gone on to Paul's house, and how Sandy had finally made up with Joe.

It sounded like more of the same. Even in Brighton, it was all a game of musical chairs, people splitting up and moving on and getting back together again. I didn't want to hear about it, not from Tony. I'd always thought of him as somehow more grown up than all the crowd at school. But that was before I knew what grown up meant.

'You're not saying much,' Tony prompted me, eventually.

'Sorry. It's been one of those days!' I sighed, wishing he'd ring off.

'With Kim? How's this romance with the local smoothie going?' he asked.

'What local smoothie?' I asked, sharply, before I could stop myself.

'That hairdresser. I thought he was a hairdresser, older guy, the usual story. . .' Tony laughed.

'I can't see what's usual about it!' I said.

'OK. . .Are you all right, Jo? It's not that you're changing your mind about seeing me up there, is it? I'll write, tonight, if it's any help. I'm nervous, too. But I haven't stopped loving you. Remember that day we went to Rottingdean. . .?' Tony reminded me.

Whenever either of us was down, the other always said, 'Remember Rottingdean?' It was a perfect summer day, a couple of years ago, and Tony's mates had organized a day out for all of us. I'd been invited, even though I was only a summer visitor, because they knew that Tony was a friend of mine. But that day the friendship had turned into something else. We'd walked side by side along the undercliff walk, just talking about this and that, and I'd been scuffing along in open-toed sandals, and had to stop when a sharp piece of shingle got stuck between my toes. One of Tony's mates had called to him, and he'd shouted back.

'Coming. Just waiting for my girl to get a stone out of her shoe. . .'

I'd been bent double brushing the stones out of my shoe, he'd been holding me steady. But when he said 'my girl', I'd looked up sharply, and almost fallen over with the suddenness of the movement. He'd caught me round the waist, and we just stood there clinging together.

'Did you mean that, about me being your girl?' I'd whispered.

'I didn't realize until I said it,' he whispered back.

And then his lips touched my cheek, softly.

'I've always loved you, Joanne,' he'd said.

And when we turned round again, all his mates were standing in a line, grinning at us both.

'So?' he'd shrugged at them, blushing. 'What's wrong with love?'

Nothing had been wrong about it then. And remembering made a lump rise in my throat, and tears welled up in my eyes. Tony was special. He was my guy, my best friend for years, someone I'd looked up to and leaned on. Was I ready to throw all that away? How could I tell him that I was falling, too quickly, for someone else?

'See you soon, love,' Tony murmured.

'See you,' I said, putting the phone down.

That night I reread all his old letters. I dragged them out of my bottom drawer, and looked through each, from the first, years ago, to the latest. And there were all the other souvenirs, crammed into that drawer, too: the fortune-telling card from the slot machine on the pier that had said, 'The man you will marry is standing next to you, now.' We'd had a good laugh about that. I'd been twelve. I'd known it was stupid. But I'd kept it, all the same.

And I'd kept the shell Tony had picked up from the beach for me when I was thirteen, and the ribbon I'd wound round my wild hair on that day we'd walked to Rottingdean, and the ticket he'd bought for us to travel back to the pier in style on the miniature railway.

Then there were the photographs, little postage-stamp sized ones taken in the booths on the sea-front, bigger out-of-focus ones I'd taken one year I got a Polaroid for Christmas, photos I'd taken laughing so hard that the camera shook, photos I'd taken secretly, creeping up on him while he sketched or threw stones into the sea, or just looked in that fixed way of his, so intently, at a pebble or a cloud, or the shape of a seagull's wing. And from all the photographs those eyes stared at me, smiling, sad, distant, too close, but always always so clear, so perfectly the colour of the sea and the clouds.

'Tony!' I cried, wiping tears from his smile. I hadn't fallen out of love with him. But something else was blotting him out.

'When's Tony coming up?' Kim asked me on Wednesday.

'Don't know yet,' I said, thinking guiltily of that letter of his that had arrived in the morning post. I hadn't wanted to open it. Not today, when I was going to see Paolo.

'Bet you can't wait!' Marie said, excitedly. 'Just think, all those Saturday nights out at the art college. They have discos every Saturday, y'know, sometimes with live groups! It's miles better than Boogy's. And all those hunky art students with earrings in one ear!'

'Earrings in one ear!' Kim snorted. 'Marie, honestly, do you like that sort of thing? Have you ever been out to the Anglers' Arms at North Alton?'

'What's that? A pub? Does your mum let you go to pubs? Mind you, I did in Spain, but it's different there, isn't it? Anyone can go into bars, and some of them are real pubs, in Benidorm, just like here, with proper English beer and. . .'

I was crunched up waiting for the next part of Kim's comments. Had Paolo taken her to the Anglers' Arms on Sunday after he'd taken me there on Saturday? How could he?

'The Anglers' Arms is a restaurant on the river, if you must know. And Paolo's taking me there, soon. We passed the place the other night, and he's promised to take me there for a meal.'

'Do they have Black Forest gateau?' Marie asked, enthusiastically.

'Yeah,' I said.

'*You've* been there?' Kim asked, frowning.

'Once,' I said.

'Oh. . .' she stammered.

'*And* she wore her earrings in one ear, didn't you, Jo?' Ellen grinned, winking at me, pleased I'd shut Kim up.

But I wasn't very pleased with myself. I'd almost given myself away.

Tony's letter was lying on the hall table when I got home. I picked it up, and then put it down again. I was too jumpy to open it. I'd been on edge since Saturday night counting the hours until I could see Paolo again. Now, it was almost time. I had to get ready. Sweatshirt and jeans wouldn't do for Paolo, because goodness knows where he'd take me, and I had to look pretty grown up. He was five years older than me, and that was a big gap to bridge. But he didn't seem to notice. He'd treated me as if those years didn't matter. . .

On second thoughts I grabbed Tony's letter on my way upstairs to change. I didn't want Mum asking questions about why I hadn't opened it. And as I made up, carefully, smudging gold shadow over my lids and across my cheekbones, I kept seeing that letter, my name in Tony's handwriting, glaring at me like an accusation.

In the end, I turned it over. What Tony didn't know wouldn't hurt him. Perhaps I wouldn't have to finish with him. If Paolo didn't finish with Kim, why should I? I'd tell him that tonight. All or nothing.

I smiled at myself. That just might work. After all, why should I go on being worried about Kim, and have to listen to her snide comments about how much she was loved? I was loved, as well. By two guys. And one of them was hers!

Chapter 7

I felt on top of the world. Paolo said, as soon as he saw me,

'Hey, you look good enough to go somewhere really special!' He stood there, his hands on my shoulders so appreciatively that it was almost embarrassing. And then his arms circled me and he kissed me slowly and smoulderingly.

Tony would've swung me round off my feet and

I'd've kicked and giggled and thumped him playfully on the shoulders and shouted, 'Put me down', and by the time he did I'd've been all sticky and messed up, and then we'd've run down the road together hand in hand.

But Paolo kissed me, and eased me into my seat, and whispered,

'I knew I was right about you!' and I felt the same way, too.

I sank back into the upholstered seat, leaning my head back and closing my eyes as he pushed a cassette into the stereo player. It wasn't the kind of music I usually went for. It was hoarse and dusky and soulful, Lionel Ritchie or someone like that, but it was the right music for the mood. The car slowed at the traffic lights in High Street, and I opened my eyes and leaned towards him to whisper some of the words of the song into his ear.

And then I slid down in the seat. Walking on the other side of High Street, and looking towards the car were Marie and Ellen, carrying their sports bags. I'd forgotten. It was badminton night. Last week's match had been cancelled, that's why I'd been able to have my hair done, but Ellen had reminded me about this game on Friday. It had slipped my mind completely.

I prayed that they hadn't seen me, and turned my back towards them, hiding behind my hair.

Paolo followed my glance as the lights changed.

'You know those two kids?' he asked.

'Yes. . .' I muttered. 'Marie and Ellen. The plump red-haired one's Marie, and Ellen's the one wearing the track suit. It's badminton night. I'm supposed to be playing!'

'Not with those two!' Paolo said.

'Why. . .why not?' I asked.

He laughed. 'I don't see it, that's all. I don't see how they can be friends of yours. They look so young.'

'They're in my class!' I argued.

'Sshhh!' Paolo whispered, smiling, touching my lips with his fingers. 'Don't say "class". Don't say "school". Don't you realize, you're not a schoolgirl to me? I don't like to think of you that way. Now Kim. . .that's different. . .'

'You're still seeing Kim?' I asked, quietly.

He shrugged and spread his hands before putting them back on the wheel.

'I try. I keep trying! I get nowhere. I say something. She cries. What can I do, Joanne? I've never hurt a girl in my life. I just don't want to hurt her. This. . . this sort of thing. . . it's never happened to me before. I don't really know how to handle it. Trust me. I know it has to be done. Tell me how to do it, Jo!'

'Wish I knew. I've got to face the problem myself. With Tony. It's going to be hard going,' I sniffed.

'Don't worry. Don't be upset. Please, Joanne. We've got time. All the time in the world. We've got until for ever,' he murmured taking my hand in his for a moment, smiling at me, gently and lovingly.

It was a kind of promise. 'All the time in the world.'

The car was filled with easy piano and strings and that haunting voice singing about love.

'Disco. Shall we go to the disco?' Paolo asked, suddenly.

'You said somewhere special! Boogy's isn't somewhere special,' I said. It was the last place I wanted to go to. Sam and Jack went there in the week, and that blond boy, Gary, from the record shop, and Angie, and Sue Fraser. I could bump into any of those.

'Boogy's? Boogy's?' Paolo asked, his voice rising in horror. 'That place should be renamed "Wallies". All the little freaks in town go in there, and litter the place with their crisp packets and their tinned shandies. Does it look to you as if we're driving to Boogy's? Look!'

He was driving down a quiet dimly-lit street in the old part of the city.

'That's where we're going!' he grinned, pulling into the kerb, and pointing to a small discreet brass plate set into the wall of what looked like just another imposing three-storey house.

'Plaisir. Members only,' the sign read.

'What is it?' I asked.

'A collar and tie disco. Wait a moment,' he said.

From the back seat he took a pale blue silk tie, fastened the top button of his striped shirt and eased himself into a navy wool jacket that had been hanging on a hook behind his seat.

'All set?' he asked.

It was really strange. I'd passed that place hundreds of times when I took a short cut from the department stores in High Street to the little shops in Cathedral Close. But I'd never noticed it. Boogy's had a big green sign that flashed on and off, and crush bars on the double doors, and a large sign saying 'The Management reserve the right to refuse admission'. And, in the evening, Mad Jack, this huge dustbin of a man, stood outside, looking as if he'd bounce Giant Haystacks if he tried to get in. Marie always said hello to Mad Jack, and he always gave her a special wink, but everyone else sidled round him, and gave him plenty of room.

There was no Mad Jack on the door of Plaisir. There was just a bell. And when Paolo pressed it, a man in a dark suit, a tall slim man with a tiny moustache, opened the door and said, 'Good evening, sir. Pleased to see you again. If you wouldn't mind signing the young lady in? Thank you very much, sir.'

I could just imagine Tony being on the receiving end of that. Or, what I mean is, I couldn't. His Guernsey sweater and cut-off jeans wouldn't go down a bomb with Mr Moustache. Come to think of it, Mr Moustache with the plummy voice was as big a threat in his well-groomed way as Mad Jack.

I had to sign a leather-bound book. And then Paolo led me down the blue-carpeted corridor to the cloakroom.

'Leave your coat in there, and freshen up. I'll wait for you here,' he said.

There was no sound of music at all from behind the leather brass-studded door that he pointed to. I trembled into the cloakroom, into a maze of mirrors and tissue dispensers, and thick carpets. For a moment, I felt as if I was back in that hairdressers.

Then I came to. I'd changed since then. A week's a long time, especially when you're with someone who takes this kind of luxury in his stride. I handed my coat to the attendant, perked up my make-up, put on a confident smile in the full length mirrors, and went out to meet Paolo.

He pushed open the leather door, and I drifted in on a cloud of music.

It was all quiet jazz-funk, and a subdued light show, in shades of blue. There were alcoves around the small circular dance floor, and a long leather-padded bar down one side of the room. Couples were dancing slinkily knee to knee, or in old fashioned ballroom clinches. There were some balding men sitting on the stools along the bar.

'Well?' Paolo asked.

'It's a funny kind of disco,' I murmured. And then I realized that had come out all wrong, as if I were saying I didn't go for it much. 'Sort of relaxing,' I added.

And it was, once I got used to it. Paolo and I found a booth to ourselves. The smooth music and the lights and the dark wood and leather upholstery made me feel as if I were out at sea, on a luxury cruise, all alone with just Paolo's dark brooding eyes for company.

He slid his arm round my waist and nuzzled my neck. His breath tickled, just under my ear, sending me muzzy inside.

'Not here,' I whispered.

'No one can see,' he whispered back.

That was true. We were shipwrecked, the two of us, on a sea of mood music. I relaxed into his kisses.

'I can't stop thinking about you, Jo!' he murmured. 'I can't get you out of my mind. Don't ever leave me!'

'I won't. I won't!' I breathed, my fingers buried in his dark soft hair.

'I need you. You know that. I'm sorry things aren't right yet, but they will be. I want it to be open, not hiding away in corners like this!' he said.

'Me, too,' I agreed.

'Let's dance,' he said.

We smooched gently to the music, my cheek against his soft cheek. I closed my eyes and dreamed. . . I'd walk into the classroom. They'd all be talking about the party on the Saturday night, and who'd finally made it with whom, and I'd drift past to Kim, who'd be sitting, as usual, on her desk, pretending not to listen, and I'd slowly raise my hand to smooth my hair back, and she'd see, and her eyes would open wider and wider and she'd say, 'But I thought you and Tony weren't. . .?' And I'd say, casually, 'Oh, the engagement ring? You noticed. Whatever made you think Tony could afford a ring like this! No. It's someone you know, actually. Remember Paolo?'

And everyone would crowd round me and want to see the ring, and want to know how and when, and Marie would turn green from the toes up and. . .

'I love you,' Paolo whispered as the music drifted away.

'Oh, Paolo!' I said, like a little kid, all full of tears.

It just didn't seem real. It didn't seem like me, crazy Joanne Farmer, sixteen, schoolgirl, five-foot-seven of stringiness, the kid who'd played hopscotch on Brighton sea-front only a fortnight ago, in denim shorts and a Snoopy t-shirt. It didn't seem like the Joanne Farmer who sat in class in a mayonnaise-splattered polo-neck and a grey skirt trying to talk sense into a computer, dissecting frogs in Biology, grappling with Advanced maths.

It didn't seem like Joanne Farmer, Kim's best mate. Tony's girlfriend.

Not here, in Paolo's arms in a disco that was pretending not to be a disco.

I was too many different people. And the person I couldn't stop being was the Joanne Farmer whose head and heart were reeling with crazy love for a crazy Italian smile.

Paolo drove me home through the city lights, but they all seemed to be dancing inside my head.

'It won't be long, Joanne,' he promised, as I slid out of the car. 'We'll both be free, soon. By this time next week, I hope? I'll see you next Wednesday?'

'Seven?'

'In the car-park. Think of me?'

'Always,' I murmured.

I floated home, the soft music still smouldering in my ears. Not like Boogy's. Not one bit like Boogy's.

Mum was waiting for me in the kitchen, watching the clock, ready to snap.

'Sorry. I'm five minutes late!' I smiled.

'Ten,' she corrected. 'Where've you been? I thought Wednesday was badminton night. Thought you had a big match on?'

'I went to the disco,' I said.

'Hmm. I told Tony you'd be at the Leisure Centre, so he went up there looking for you, and then came back and no one up there had seen you either,' she said.

'Tony!' I gasped. 'What's he doing here?'

'You know very well what he's doing here. A foundation course in art. And he told you in his letter that he'd been offered a room in college, and that he'd decided to move in tonight,' Mum said, folding her arms, the way she always did when I'd annoyed her.

'I. . . I haven't had time to read his letter,' I muttered, half to myself.

'And from the look of your room, you haven't had time to tidy that. And what about your homework? I don't know, Joanne. In the last week or so you've been impossible! And now you've upset Tony. . .'

'Have I?' I stammered.

'Of course you have! Wouldn't you be upset if you arrived in a strange town, to see your girlfriend, and she'd gone out, goodness knows where? He said to tell you he'll be at the college tomorrow, near the notice board, at quarter past four. I've passed the message on, and that's all I can do. I'm not asking any questions. But think about what you're doing. That's all. As long as you know, I don't need to. But *do* you know? I'm not sure that you do, any more!' she said, frowning.

I wiped my eyes with the back of my hand.

'I'll go up to bed, then,' I said.

The bubble had burst. Tony was here.

I dragged up the stairs to my room, took the letter from my dressing table, and read it.

Dearest Jo, it said. I can't make out what seems to be wrong with you. I only know I'm worried. So I've taken one of the college residence rooms, and I'm coming tomorrow (Wednesday). I don't know whether I'll be much use to you up there, but I know I'm no use to anyone here, thinking about you all the time.

There's a chance that you don't want me at all, now you've had time to think about it. If that's how you feel, please tell me on Wednesday. I'll understand. I don't want to push you.

And please don't worry about Kim. It'll all blow over, soon.

I love you. See you Wednesday. Tony.

Just another letter to cry over.

Chapter 8

Talk about jungle drums! Just when I wanted to be on my own, and think things over, the school gossip service had thundered into full production. Everyone from the first years up must've been at the Leisure

Centre on Wednesday night, because people I didn't even know came up to me all day Thursday telling me that this hunky-looking boy had been looking for me at the badminton match, asking if that was my famous art student boyfriend from Brighton, and if so did he have any mates, and were there any parties up at the college?

By lunchtime I was in a mood to cut throats. I tried to hide in the computer room, and catch up with some of my neglected homework, but thoughts of Paolo and Tony kept getting in the way of the keyboard.

Marie and Ellen tracked me down. I'd been avoiding them all morning, which wasn't too difficult, because they had Social Science Community option on Thursday mornings which took them out of school at half-past nine, and they didn't reappear until one o'clock.

'She's in here, Kim,' Marie yelled down the corridor.

That was all I needed.

Kim had been on at me on the bus that morning and I'd had to build lie on lie to explain to her why I hadn't been at the badminton match, and where I was.

'Got a bone to pick with you!' Ellen said, pulling up the chair next to me. 'Star player does a bunk on the night of the Big Match.'

'Sorry. I just forgot. . .' I mumbled, blushing.

'And then there's the sudden appearance of the confused boyfriend. . .' Ellen continued.

'I forgot about him, too. . .'

Ellen raised her eyebrows as only Ellen can do.

'Did you go for another hair appointment?' Marie giggled. 'I never did get the full story of what happened last time. Did you see the famous Paolo?'

'We're not talking about him, just at the moment. We're talking about Joanne's mysterious lapses of memory,' Ellen said, saving me, because just at that moment Kim walked in, too. 'Where *did* you go, last night?'

'Doctor's,' I muttered.

'That stomach upset?' Marie asked.

I nodded. The lies were starting to upset my stomach yet again.

'You can wait hours at the health centre. . .' Marie said, sympathetically, with just a quick glance at Ellen.

I couldn't make out whether they'd seen me in Paolo's car or not. Neither of them was letting on. I was walking on very thin ice.

Marie pulled up a chair on the other side of me. Kim perched on the bench-top at the back of the room, pulled out an emery board from the pocket of her skirt and started sawing at her nails. The sound went right through me.

'So?' Marie breathed.

'So?' I asked.

'So now we've seen what you've been keeping to yourself for all this time, we're dead impressed,' she said.

'What d'you mean?' I jumped.

'Tony. Thought you said he was "nice". I expected someone who looked like spotty Sam without the spots. But when I saw him – I could scratch your eyes out, Jo Farmer!' Marie said, enviously.

'And, to get to the point, Marie and I want to know when you're seeing him again, and when we're getting our invite to meet him properly?' Ellen smiled.

'Lee's not going to be too chuffed about that!' I grinned back.

'Finished. Last night. I'm a victim of the start of the soccer season,' she said with a half smile that didn't quite come off.

'So Ellen's on the loose, and I'm on the loose, as usual, and we're both on the look-out for a more sophisticated type of guy, the older man, y'know, like Kim's guy,' Marie giggled. Kim glared.

'Art students,' Ellen said.

'Like yours, if possible,' Marie added.

They were both crushing me in.

'This sounds like blackmail,' I said, jokingly.

'Could be!' Marie winked.

I swallowed, hard.

'I'm. . . supposed to be meeting Tony after school, in the main college building. . .'

'Right. Don't mind if we tag along? I knew you wouldn't! Great!' Marie crowed.

'What about you, Kim?' Ellen asked over her shoulder.

'Doesn't sound as if I'm invited,' Kim said, coldly.

'I don't remember inviting these two either!' I said. 'But if you want to come along, you're welcome, Kim.'

It wasn't a bad idea. Turning up there with mates would take a bit of the pressure off me.

'I'm expecting a phone call, tonight,' Kim said, jumping from the bench, and walking towards the door. 'I've already found the guy I want, haven't I?'

She closed the door behind herself as she waltzed out.

'Get her!' Marie flounced.

'Moody as hell. One minute she's OK, and the next she's unbearable. I can't make her out,' Ellen grumbled.

'Did you meet this boyfriend, Jo? When you went to have your hair done? What's he like?' Marie asked.

I shrugged, and hoped that the blush didn't show, or the terrible guilt that was causing it.

'I didn't see much of him. But he wasn't as bad as I expected,' I muttered.

'You can't judge by what someone looks like. He must be a pretty weird guy to have that effect on Kim,' Ellen murmured.

'Maybe he's hypnotizing her! Maybe he's got her in his power. Maybe she's not Kim at all. Maybe she's just this programmed robot that. . .' Marie fantasized.

'Yeah, I read that book, too,' Ellen said, sourly. 'C'mon, Marie. Let's get you out of this computer room before it turns what's left of your brain!'

She linked arms with Marie, and took her out, grumbling.

'See you at home-time,' she called to me, leaving me staring at the computer wondering whether I could programme it to sort me out.

*

I couldn't get out of it. Marie and Ellen were dead keen. Marie never stopped rabbiting from the moment we left school. Ellen didn't say much. She was probably thinking about Lee. The break-up was probably hurting more than she was showing.

The art college was on the edge of the city centre, a tall blackened building in red and yellow brick, very ugly. We took a short cut through the back streets to get there, and passed the Plaisir disco on the way. It really did exist. It hadn't been a dream. All that crazy feeling, last night, with Paolo, the whispered promises about a future together, they must've been real, too. In the watery September afternoon sunlight, the magic of last night's mood had been washed away. I was Jo Farmer, schoolgirl, again, tramping through town in my school uniform with my mates.

We walked up the huge stone steps to the main entrance in silence. Marie was all wide-eyed, as if she were taking a step into a new world.

I saw Tony immediately. His back was towards us, and he was deep in conversation with another student, but the set of his shoulders, the way he stood with all his weight on one leg, leaning slightly to the right, his head on one side, brought this great surge of familiarity and love that made me want to call out and run to him and have him swing me round again.

He turned.

'Jo!' he said, walking quickly towards me, his soft eyes all bright, that funny smile lighting up his face.

'Hi, Tony!' I breathed, taking hold of both his hands. For a moment, no one else existed.

'You were out, last night,' he said.

'Sorry. Unavoidable. I'll explain later,' I stammered. 'But I'm here now.'

'And. . . Kim?' Tony said, looking first at Marie, then at Ellen.

'No. This is Marie, and Ellen. They wanted to meet you properly. They were playing badminton last night, when you went round to the Leisure Centre.'

'Oh, I remember!' he grinned.

'We've come to be introduced to a better class of boy,' Marie said. 'I fancy these arty types. I went out with one once. I think his name was Rolf. You've not bumped into a Rolf yet, have you?'

'Don't think so!' Tony laughed, taking my hand. 'But I'm a bit at sea myself yet. I. . . I think I can find the coffee bar, with a bit of luck. Coming?'

Marie was dazed, staring at all the huge canvasses displayed on the walls. Even Ellen seemed impressed. And, in a way, I was. It was better than our school, and it didn't smell as bad as the Leisure Centre. I liked the paintings. My mind flicked back to those phoney hunting prints on the walls at the Angler's Arms. But that was different. It was a pub, and the prints had fitted in, somehow.

The coffee bar was a high-ceilinged room with low scuffed coffee tables, and the usual mess of plastic cups. It was quieter and not as chaotic as the coffee bar in the Leisure Centre, but it gave me the same sinking feeling.

'Fantastic!' Marie said, looking round at the carefully mounted displays of students' work on the walls, and at the students lounging about on the battered cloth chairs. 'Isn't your Tony lovely, Joanne? You aren't half lucky!'

Tony came back with coffees, and with a couple of other students in tow. He introduced them, Sean and Lewis who were in the same block of rooms as he was. Marie started jabbering away to Lewis.

'How's things?' Tony murmured to me.

'OK,' I sighed.

'Last night?'

'Oh. You know. I'm still rushing round trying to sort Kim out,' I stammered.

Tony squeezed my hand.

'Don't you think she can look after herself?' he asked, gently. 'You look a bit strained.'

'I'm OK. I'll be OK, soon, anyway. And you? How's the settling in?' I asked. I felt as if we were two strangers, carefully examining each other, trying not to put a foot wrong. All the silly laughter of the Brighton days had gone. Was the love still there?

'It's going to be the best thing I ever did, I reckon,' he smiled. 'Mum and Dad wanted me to stay round Brighton, but I needed a change of scene. I just hope it doesn't muck things up between us, love.'

'Why should it?' I snapped.

'A dance! Wow!' Marie shouted, into my left ear.

'Oh yeah. Meant to ask you. There's a disco here on Saturday, in the coffee bar. They clear all the tables out, and decorate the place up, it's supposed to be good. Coming?' Tony grinned.

'Yeah. . .' I said, trying to find the right mood to sound enthusiastic.

'And don't dress up! Not that you would, anyway,

but I'm warning you, just in case. "Informal dress" it says, so Snoopy shirt and jeans'll do fine.'

'Right,' I muttered. Even for Boogy's you could dress up a bit. But this was a different world even from Boogy's. I wanted to enjoy it. I'd looked forward to it so much. But too many things had happened.

Tony walked us all back across town to the bus station. Marie and Ellen walked in front of us, but kept glancing at us slyly, over their shoulders. They needn't've bothered. We weren't doing anything. I was chatting, answering his questions and all that, but in the back of my mind I kept wondering whether Paolo had phoned Kim, and whether she was seeing him that night, and whether I could wait until Wednesday to see him again.

Tony was an old friend, that was all. More like a big brother, really, with his bits of advice, and gentle hints about what I should and shouldn't do. Holding his hand meant nothing, and even the goodbye kiss at the bus-stop didn't ring any bells. It was gentle, brotherly. It didn't get inside me and shake me up.

Marie and Ellen, all of a giggle, got off the bus at the Pear-tree Garage. And I got off at the next stop, the one by Kim's. I walked up and down outside her house two or three times. I wanted to go in, and see her, and settle this thing once and for all. All I had to say was, 'Paolo loves me. Not you.' I could come right out with the truth, and then settle up with Tony, somehow, and get my life sorted out into a new pattern.

But, in the end, I just hadn't got the nerve. I walked

back home, praying that I wouldn't see a white Cortina estate heading towards Kim's house.

I didn't. But that didn't stop me thinking about it, and imagining the scene where we had a big show-down, and Paolo walked away with me.

Chapter 9

I went out on Saturday and bought myself a new t-shirt in the sales. And I bought some henna, too, and spent the whole afternoon walking round the house with my hair plastered to my head with the sticky yellow clay.

I'd decided, you see. I'd decided that if Paolo had settled into the wait-and-see scene, I could do the same. I'd make up to Tony. I'd posh up for him, and remember the good times, and make the most of being at the dance with him, and then tell Paolo all about it, and try to make him as jealous as I was feeling.

Kim had been full of it on Friday, about Paolo's phone call and about how crazy he was to see her, and how they were going out for the whole day on Saturday, to drive along the coast and eat at this seafood restaurant that Paolo knew about.

When she'd told me, I'd smiled inside. I knew that it had to be the last scene in Kim's little drama. But the doubts had started on Friday night. She wouldn't let him go. She'd turn on the tears, and he'd be hooked again, and on Wednesday he'd be as depressed as ever, asking me what he was supposed to do. . .

Well, he didn't know about the art college dance, or that Tony had arrived. Kim might tell him, because she'd been a bit ruffled that Ellen and Marie and I had been invited, but maybe she never mentioned me to him. She had no reason to, now.

So I could tell him myself, and lay it on with a trowel about how great the dance had been, and how much I'd enjoyed myself.

Who was I kidding? I couldn't do that to Paolo. He hadn't deserved it. It wasn't his fault that I felt lonely and deserted all Saturday. It wasn't his fault that Kim was so clinging. He had a real problem with her. With Tony, I could just say, 'I've changed my mind,' and he'd take it. One thing about Tony, he'd never crowded me. If I wanted to finish it, I could do it. Of course I could. And I would finish it, for Paolo. He was everything Tony was, but much much more. Maybe Tony understood that I needed a special kind of treatment.

By the time I went to meet Ellen and Marie at the Pear-tree Garage, I was as confused as ever. But I looked OK. I looked quite good, really.

And so did Marie and Ellen. Marie had her tight pink jeans and pink over-shirt on, which clashed horribly with her hair, but she could get away with it. Ellen was all in black, black tight skirt, black tights, black t-shirt. Dramatic. They were both really excited the way I always was just before a date with Paolo. Always? There'd only been two dates. But a lot can happen in two dates.

When we got on the bus, I noticed Ellen had gold sleepers in her ears.

'You've had your ears pierced!' I said.

'Today. I celebrated,' she grinned.

'What were you celebrating?' I asked.

'Finishing with Lee. I've wanted to get my ears pierced all summer, but he said it was too dangerous. He said that if I got into a fight at a soccer match some girl could grab, hold of my earrings and tear them out and mess up my earlobes for life. He said it'd happened to one of his girlfriends once.'

I shuddered. 'Can't imagine it!' I said.

'Me neither. Thought'd never crossed my mind. If I saw a fight at a soccer match I'd run a mile in the opposite direction!' Ellen agreed.

'D'you miss him? Lee?' I asked. She'd seemed so close to him. They looked a good couple, plenty of laughs, all that sort of thing. A bit like me and Tony, really.

'In a way. But he was soccer mad, a real fanatic. It got me down. Who wants to stand all Saturday morning watching him play in the school soccer team, then all Saturday afternoon watching City play, then hold his hand all Saturday night at the Leisure Centre while he goes through every one of the moves of both matches with his stupid mates? Even at Mandy's party, he was on about football all night. I couldn't stand it any more. Time to move on, eh?' she grinned. 'Time I got treated like a lady!'

'Some chance you've got!' Marie teased.

'Some chance any of us've got, but at least we're moving up in the world, now, aren't we? That art college looks great. Makes a change from the Leisure Centre!' Ellen said.

'I like the Leisure Centre!' Marie said hotly. 'Mind you, I don't mind moving up in the world, either. I reckon I could get a taste for art, if I tried hard. And did you see the way that Sean looked at me? Don't you think he's got nice teeth?'

'All the better to eat you with, my dear!' Ellen said, in a Little Red Riding Hood wolf's voice.

Marie started hooting and screeching with laughter and everyone on the bus was staring at us when we jumped off outside the art college. I felt a bit embarrassed. I hadn't noticed much before what a piercing laugh Marie had. It went right through me.

But once she'd started, she couldn't stop, and Ellen got the giggles, too. She kept nudging Marie and telling her to shut up, and then both of them went into fits again.

Tony looked at me, and then at the two of them as we walked up. He looked scruffily attractive in a softly checked dark shirt with the sleeves rolled up, and his old jeans, and that Brighton tan.

'Didn't you get the joke?' he asked me. 'Something's obviously tickled those two.'

'Oh, they're just in one of those moods!' I said.

I wished they'd shut up. People were looking at us, and probably remembering that we were the three schoolgirls who'd turned up in school uniforms at the coffee bar on Thursday. I wanted to pretend I wasn't a schoolgirl at all. With Paolo, I could manage it, but I couldn't in this crowd, especially with Tony encouraging them, by making Ellen do the wolf voice for him. She was a good mimic, and she did the wolf with a thick Devon accent. It had Tony giggling in no time.

I felt left out.

The coffee bar had been transformed, with hunks of stage scenery, huge forest scenes, set up against and sticking out from the walls, and mock-ups of real trees grouped around the coffee bar counter. That put a stop to Marie's laughter, and Ellen's giggles. It was pretty impressive.

'Wow!' Marie breathed.

'Good, isn't it?' Tony smiled. 'I helped. I lugged three of those trees up from the basement myself. We all helped. The lads told me that they go to this trouble for all the discos.'

'It's better than Boogy's, even,' Ellen said.

The sound system was pretty good, too, and the DJ, one of the students, who kept the records going with plenty of disco tracks and a few oldies. In one of my better moods, I'd have thrown myself into the party spirit with the same wild enthusiasm Marie and Ellen were showing. I felt happy enough, in a way. But there were the doubts, there was the guilt, there was the constant feeling of wanting to be somewhere else.

I was starting to look and sound like Kim. I really didn't want to be like her. All I wanted was Paolo, and he wasn't here. He probably wouldn't be seen dead here.

'You've done a great job,' I smiled at Tony.

'Glad you approve,' he said, bowing jokingly.

Marie and Ellen, though, were really getting on my nerves. They were being all stupid, giggly and whispering every time someone spoke to them. Maybe, if we'd been on our own, I'd have had a chance to say something to him about Paolo. I wanted to bring the subject up, just to clear the air. But it wasn't the time or the place.

Marie finally went off to dance with Ellen at the edge of the dance floor. They looked as if they were working their way round to where Sean and Lewis were sitting with a crowd of other students. Marie was bumping and grinding, as she usually did, and Ellen was trying to be smooth and cool, but she kept laughing at Marie's antics. I knew they didn't have a chance. They were far too obvious.

Tony and I stood by the bar, sipping our cokes, and watching their progress. Then, suddenly, the DJ put on a real oldie, a Buddy Holly number, 'Rave On'. Tony looked at me, and twinkled.

'Shall we?' he asked.

I hung back for a moment. Tony'd had this thing about old fifties and sixties records for as long as I'd known him, and over the years he'd built up a huge collection. And he'd taught me to rock, old style. It had taken him ages to get me to understand the footwork, but after a few years of summer holidays and practice, we'd got to the stage where rock'n roll was our Brighton party-piece. No one here knew about it. I'd never imagined that we'd be able to dance together up here. I didn't know whether

I wanted to, the mood I was in, or whether I dared.

'I'm not dressed for it. . .' I hesitated.

'Aw c'mon. Never mind the gear. It'll be a laugh, even in jeans and trainers,' Tony said, pulling me on to the dance floor.

It was one of the odd funny things about Tony that I'd always loved. He was shy and didn't like making an exhibition of himself, but some things, like old rock music, brought him out of his private world with its private jokes and private smiles, and he didn't care what people thought or said about what he did. Like the time he'd told that mob in Brighton that he loved me. It was the same sort of unexpected confidence.

The music took him over. And me, too. Dancing with him, I forgot the chaotic emotions that were churning inside me, battling with each other. I just slipped into the rhythm, took my lead from him, and lost myself.

I hardly noticed the other dancers making room for us, and then crowding round to watch us. I hardly noticed the change of record to another of Tony's favourites, Elvis's 'Jailhouse Rock', or the wild applause for all our big production numbers. It was just old Tony and old Jo, doing their party piece, and loving it.

And then the music ended, and there was a brief silence, before the place erupted in foot-stamping and clapping, and all for us. Tony held my clammy hand.

'Thanks Jo!' he panted. 'See? The old team can still make good!'

Marie and Ellen were clamouring up.

'What d'you mean by that?' I asked him, nervously.

'Come on. I know you,' he murmured. 'I've known you since you were this high. I know something's wrong. But that was good. So maybe the old magic's still alive somewhere. . . I'll get us some more cokes. You look as if you need one, and I feel as if *I* need one.'

I could've gone after him, and asked him to carry on that conversation instead of running away, but Marie and Ellen grabbed me.

'I didn't know you could dance like that, Jo Farmer!' Marie said enviously.

'And isn't Tony fantastic? I've never seen real rock'n'roll like that, except on telly,' Ellen added. 'I can't get over the way you two dance.'

I didn't know what to say to them. I brushed my damp hair out of my face with my fingers and looked down at my sodden t-shirt.

'Still, you're a great one for secrets!' Marie said.

'What secrets?' Tony asked, appearing suddenly.

I jumped.

'This dancing,' Marie grinned. 'And you, Tony, for a start! We'll tell you the rest of Joanne's secrets as we get to know them. She's a bit of a dark horse. You'll have to watch her y'know.'

'Let's dance, Marie,' Ellen interrupted her, quickly, dragging her off.

Tony looked down at his glass, and then up at me.

'As I was saying. . .' he murmured. 'I reckon you're keeping secrets from me. I don't know what they are, and I don't want to know. Unless you want to tell me?'

'No. . . I. . .' I stammered.

'But I think I've got to give you a breathing space. I should've asked you, before I wrote off here, if you wanted me to try for a place. I just broke the news to you when it was all settled. Maybe that was too much. Maybe you didn't really like being put in the position of having to accept it?'

'That's not the problem. . .' I sniffed.

'Jo, it might be. It just might be. So. . . I've got some settling in to do at college. I've got some work I'd like to get on with. I'll give you time to settle down, too. When you're ready to tell me outright how you feel, and what you want to do next, I'll be here. Just take a week or so to think about whether you want this to continue, this thing between us. . .'

'Tony. . .' I said, tearfully.

He wiped away the tears with his fingertips.

'It's for the best, Jo. A week's break could be what you need. Don't cry. I'm still the same. I'm not the one with problems. The only problem I have is trying to get close to you at the moment.'

'I want to tell you. . .' I sobbed.

'Not now. Leave it. Let it be. Take things easy, Jo, please,' he whispered, kissing the tip of my nose. 'Now I'll see you three to the bus-stop. We won't mention this in front of your mates. OK?'

'OK,' I agreed.

A week or two. In a week or two he was hoping

that my mind would clear and I'd love him again. I couldn't help feeling that I'd already made my decision about the one I loved. I only wished it could be Tony.

Chapter 10

I did something on Sunday that I hadn't done since before the summer holidays, I called round at Ellen's and asked her if she wanted to come to the Fun Swim at the Leisure Centre with me. She looked as surprised by my sudden enthusiasm for Sunday afternoon swimming as I was, but she collected her gear together anyway, and then we called for Marie, and finally for Kim.

Kim was the most surprised of all, and I honestly didn't expect her to come. But she was dead keen. She seemed in a funny quiet mood, not uppity at all, more thoughtful, as if she was trying to work something out, and our unexpected invitation had given her a chance to stop brooding over it for awhile. I couldn't help feeling that Paolo must have said something to her, finally. But he obviously hadn't mentioned my name, because she wasn't at all off with me.

Marie and Ellen were going on and on about the art college disco, exaggerating like mad about how great it was, and how many guys had chatted them up, and really raving about Tony.

That's when my mood started to change. I'd woken up feeling this enormous sense of relief that Tony had suggested a week's break, and hinted that he thought I wanted to finish with him. I'd felt more relaxed about the whole messy situation, and ready to turn my mind away from it, and go mad with the kids in the pool, splash about and be stupid for a change.

But Marie and Ellen got on to the subject of Tony, and the dark clouds started to roll in again.

'Have *you* met him, Kim?' Marie asked, knowing very well that she hadn't

'You ought to!' Marie went on. 'Being as you're the sort of girl who goes for these older guys! He's really funny, and fantastic looking, and you should've seen him and Joanne doing rock'n'roll. It'd bring the house down at Boogy's. And all these girls round us were eyeing him up, and going on about him, and I wanted to tell them they had no chance, 'cos that was my mate he was dancing with, and they'd been going out with each other for ever. They all fancied him, didn't they, Ellen?'

'Don't we all?' Ellen laughed. 'Just say the word when you're fed up with him, Jo, and I'll fight Marie for him!'

'Start fighting now, then, 'cos we're about to have a trial separation, y'know, go our own way for a week or two to see how things work out. . .' I said, as lightly as I could.

Ellen stopped dead in her tracks for a moment, and stared at me.

'You're kidding!' she breathed.

'Aw, Joanne! Why didn't you say before I started letting rip with my big mouth?' Marie asked, her voice heavy with real sympathy. 'I'm sorry. Really I am. I thought you two were set up for life. It's those girl art students isn't it? They're dead glam, they are. You must be feeling terrible about it!'

'It's only temporary, probably,' I tried to laugh.

'It's what film stars do, isn't it? Just before they get a divorce. It's always in the Sunday papers that they're having a trial separation and then. . .' Kim said, innocently.

'And you can shut up, Kim Saunders! Jo doesn't want her nose rubbed in it. You've not seen her Tony. You don't realize!' Ellen snorted.

'Sorry. . .' Kim stammered.

'Look. It's OK. Don't all make such a heavy deal of it!' I flared. I couldn't get over the fact that they were all assuming that Tony had finished with *me*. If only they knew! Well, they would, in time. 'I'm OK. I was quite happy about it until you started on!'

'Sorry I spoke!' Ellen huffed.

'Don't be like that, Ellie!' Marie said quietly, nudging her.

The two of them walked in front, through the doors of the Leisure Centre, Marie making faces at Ellen.

'Is that right? Has Tony really finished with you?' Kim asked, in a nervous whisper.

'No!' I sighed. 'They've got it all wrong, as usual. It's just a break. I need a break from him. I needed a bit of time to get used to the idea of him coming up here. Maybe I'll finish with him in the end, maybe I won't. I dunno!'

But what if Ellen and Marie were right? What if Tony had his eye on one of the other students? I'd never thought of that. Could I bear it if he told me it was all over, because he'd fallen for someone else?

'Oh,' Kim murmured. 'It hurts, whichever way round it happens, I suppose. I hope it doesn't finish. I don't like the thought of things finishing. Is he. . . is he getting a bit pushy. Is that the problem?'

'Pushy? How? Tony? Never!' I laughed.

'Just wondered,' she said.

I tried to forget about it all, and just have a few laughs, like we used to, all four of us, right at the beginning of the summer. In no time Marie was her usual giggly self, pushing all the guys she could see into the pool, and then diving in and swimming away from them with her amazing crawl stroke, a converted doggy paddle that made her look as if she had six arms.

Ellen relaxed too, and pulled us on to the huge airbed that always floated around at Fun Swim sessions. But Kim kept swimming off to play with some of the little kids in the shallow end, so the two of us were left sculling round on the airbed, playing dodgems with the kids on the smaller airbeds. Then I went into the diving pool, to see whether I could still manage the jump from the top board, and some huge hulking idiot started annoying me, trying to push me, and then trying to persuade me to hold hands with him and jump off in a twosome. I escaped, finally, and went to join Kim and the kids.

It wasn't too bad. For half an hour or so, I didn't think about Paolo or Tony, or about the way the four of us were changing, moving apart, getting on each other's nerves, growing up at different rates.

That feeling homed in on me afterwards, on Sunday night, and I suddenly wanted to see Paolo, before Wednesday, to cry on him, and to tell him that Tony and I were half-way to finishing, and to ask him how he'd managed with Kim. It sounded, to me, looking back, as if Kim had been trying to tell me something, or ask me something that afternoon, but I couldn't work out what.

I had to see Paolo. I had to. I couldn't wait till Wednesday.

By home time on Monday, I was desperate. Marie and Ellen had been telling everyone about the art college disco all day, but only behind my back. Whenever I came near, there was this awful buzzing quiet of one of them shushing the other, because they still thought I'd get upset if I heard Tony's name mentioned. And they were probably spreading it around that we were splitting up.

I had to tell someone the true story before I burst with frustration. And that someone could only be Paolo. He'd be so pleased. He'd know what a relief it was for me. He'd fold me against that soft crumpled leather of his jacket, and wind his fingers in my hair, and whisper.

'We're almost there, Jo. Almost free.'

I could hear him saying it. I could almost feel again the shock of his lips against mine. I had to go to the salon. It was the only thing to do. I dashed home, straight after school, and changed. Luckily for me, Kim had to go into town after school, so I didn't have to wait round for her, and I caught the early bus. I spun Mum some story about going to Kim's to get a book for my homework, shovelled down my tea, caught the five-past-five bus into town, and reached the salon at half-past. Closing time.

I waited, sheltering in the doorway of the florist's opposite impatient with happiness, watching the front door of the salon, and Paolo's car parked in the side street next to it, ready to dash across to him as soon as I saw him.

All the girls came out first, looking quite ordinary in their street clothes, and then Paolo, about ten minutes later.

With Kim.

His arm was round her shoulders. She was crying, looking up into his burning dark eyes. I turned away from them, trying to catch their reflection in the mirror tiles behind the displays of dried flowers in the shop window. I prayed that they wouldn't see me, not at that moment, not when it was so obvious that he was breaking the bad news to her.

An inner circle bus stopped at the traffic lights cutting off my view of them as they walked to the car. I jumped on it and peered through the side window of the bus, trying to get a better view of what was going on, but the traffic was lining both sides of the street, and blocked my view. Then, as the traffic pulled away, so did my bus, and I was whisked away to the next stop, on the wrong side of town before I had a chance to jump off.

Still, at least I knew that I could rest easy, now. It was all coming right, as I'd hoped it would. Paolo and I were meant to be together. Obviously.

Kim stayed off school on Tuesday and Wednesday, and when I called to see her, her mum said she was probably coming down with a virus, so I'd better not go in. Her mum and dad were always like that, making you stand on the doorstep like a stranger. Her mum had had new carpets six months ago, and wouldn't let Kim in unless she took her shoes off. But they'd been funny ever since Carl was killed, so I didn't insist on seeing her, even though I knew what she was in bed with. Heartache.

I'd make it up with her, I promised myself. We'd been good mates in the past. She'd understand, slowly, about Paolo and me. I'd find a way to help her to understand.

But, meanwhile, I had a dream come true. On Wednesday I couldn't keep the silly smile off my face and Marie got the wrong end of the stick, and asked me if Tony and I had made up. I said I'd tell her the whole story soon, and she went running off, all excited to tell Ellen and Sue Fraser and Mandy and Angie and anyone else she could find.

That silly smile was still firmly in place as I ran to the car-park that night to meet Paolo, for the very last of the secret meetings. From now on, everyone could know about us.

'You've told Kim, haven't you?' I breathed, as soon as I'd recovered from his first crazy kiss.

'What makes you say that?' he teased, opening the car door for me.

I closed the car door, quietly but firmly, without getting in, and leaned on the car, facing him.

'We can go for a walk by the river, and you can tell me all about it!' I laughed, stretching up on tiptoe to kiss his cheek. 'I love you. I really do love you! I love you more than Snoopy, more than Brighton beach, more than summer, more than my first pair of roller skates, more than the skin off the custard!'

'What's got into you?' he asked, joining in the laughter, weakly, shaking his head. He ruffled my hair. 'What's all this about?' he asked.

'Tell me you love me, too!' I insisted, stretching up to stroke his cheek, and run my fingertips across his lips.

'I love you,' he whispered, so tenderly that the giggles dried up in my mouth.

'And not Kim?' I asked.

'And not Kim. You know not Kim, Jo, you know. . . You and I, we're different. I can talk to you. You seem to understand everything I say, everything I think. . . Get into the car, Joanne. I'll take you for a drive, and we can watch a sunset. I want to talk to you, and. . .'

'Talk to me now. Let's walk by the river. Tell me how you broke the news to Kim. Was she very upset? Is she going to be OK? D'you think she'll get used to the idea of you and me in the end?' I asked.

Paolo ran his fingers through his hair. He looked confused, or impatient, or both.

'What's she been saying to you? What's Kim been saying?' he asked.

'N. . . nothing,' I stammered. 'I haven't seen her. She's been off school since Monday night. . .'

'Oh,' he muttered.

'But. . . I thought. . .' I said. I couldn't tell him that I'd been spying on the break-up scene.

'Listen, Jo. It's not going to be as easy as you think. I told you. I'm taking my time with this. I haven't got anywhere with her yet. But I will. She gets upset so easily. It's difficult,' he murmured, pulling me towards him. 'Come on. Let's go for a drive,' he whispered, rubbing his lips against my ear.

My eyes filled with tears. So I'd been wrong. I hadn't seen a break-up. I'd just seen Kim, clinging old Kim, doing another of her self-pity acts. I sniffed back the tears. I wasn't going to cry.

'I'd better get my big scene going with Tony again, then, hadn't I?' I grinned cheekily, putting a brave face on it.

'What the hell's that supposed to be? Blackmail?' he exploded, breaking my hold on his shoulders. 'You kids're all the same, up one minute, down the next, saying one thing, saying another. Can't you make your mind up what it is you want? You come here, all smiles and kisses, and then I get the third-degree, and then the threats! What're you doing to me?'

My hands dropped to my sides. Was this really Paolo, the Paolo I'd dreamed about, ached for, planned a future with? He looked cold, vicious, not the guy who'd told me a minute ago how well we understood each other. . .

'Jo, I'm sorry!' he said, breaking down and burying

his face in my hair. 'It's just that I can't stand much more. I love you so much, and it's tearing me apart, not knowing what to do next. I don't want to hurt Kim. And you don't either. But I need you! Please, Jo. I'm sorry!'

'OK,' I whispered, touching his hair lightly.

His kiss was working its old magic. I believed his kiss. Everything he was trying to tell me was there, without stupid words. Of course he loved me. No one could make me feel so helplessly crazy inside without loving me.

'I'll take you to the Anglers' Arms,' he promised.

'I have to be in early. I've got some biology to write up, and Mum's been on at me. That's why I asked you just to come down the river for a walk. I'm sorry, Paolo. I've got to go,' I trembled.

'I've got to see you again, soon. When? Friday? Sunday?' he asked.

'Why not Saturday?' I dared to argue.

'London. I'm going to London,' he muttered.

'Friday, then,' I said.

'Same time? Here?' he asked.

I nodded.

'How long's it going to be like this, Paolo?' I asked, wearily.

'Hold on, just a bit longer, Jo. Just a bit longer. . .' he said.

Chapter 11

Just a bit longer. . .

I wasn't sure exactly what that meant. Days? Months? Meanwhile, there were a lot of lies to tell.

I watched Paolo's car pull out of the car-park that night, glanced up at the clock on the Co-op tower, and saw that I could still make it. I ran out of the car-park, picking up my sports bag from the bench in the park, where it had been guarded by a pensioner who always sat there in the evenings watching his Jack Russell chasing the leaves.

'Thanks!' I told him.

'Quite all right, my dear!' he smiled.

I had to run all the way to the Leisure Centre, too, and change in five minutes flat, but at least I'd got there, at least there'd be no questions or whispers or secret comments about the funny way I was behaving.

'Well well well, look who it isn't!' Ellen smirked when I appeared at the side of the badminton court, but I could see that she was genuinely pleased that I hadn't let the team down again.

I couldn't tell Paolo that I had to play a badminton match. I'd had to spin him that story about the home-work. After his outburst about kids and mind-chan-ging and up and down emotions, how could I say that my mates were counting on me, and that I preferred playing a badminton match to going to the Anglers' Arms?

I didn't. I'd wanted to sit and watch the sunset, chat about things, look through that window at the river and the swans, but there'd've been too much hassle in keeping Marie and Ellen sweet if I'd done that. These days, there was always something I'd rather be doing, than whatever it was I was doing, always a nagging feeling dragging me down like a badly filled back tooth.

I played badminton better than ever, though, attacking that shuttlecock as if I'd got something personal against it. I was playing doubles, with Sue Fraser as my partner, and she kept looking at me out of the corner of her eye as I put smash after smash away.

'What's your mum been putting in your cocoa? Iron pills?' she asked, all amazed, after we'd clobbered the pair we were playing against.

We were the only winners from our team, and Ellen insisted on buying me a coke to celebrate. I felt high on success. No one mentioned Tony. No one was feeling sorry for me. No one was pussy-footing round me. It was a good feeling, being a winner, and not being envied for it, and not having to cheat to get there.

But by Friday, that good uncomplicated feeling had evaporated. I was all on edge, getting ready to see Paolo. I dawdled, running through in my mind, all the arguments for calling it a day, and pulling out of this crazy romance. But I knew I'd be there, all the same, on the car-park, ready for more of the same.

I was just wiping the tears away so that I could put some mascara on, when Mum shouted up the stairs to me that Kim was here, and that she was sending her up. Just what I needed!

'Your mum said you might be going out. . .' she stammered, stepping into my room nervously.

There were three LPs under her arm, and she was carrying a plastic carrier bag. It looked as if she'd planned on staying for a while. I knew what was in that carrier bag. It was the cotton two-piece that she'd been making for herself on my sewing machine before the summer holidays.

'I. . . I thought you were in bed with a mysterious virus,' I said. She hadn't been back at school since that Monday night I'd seen her with Paolo, and he'd put me right on my heartache theory.

'Yeah. I was. I'm a bit run down, I reckon,' she laughed, hollowly. 'But I had to get up today. I'm supposed to be seeing Paolo tomorrow night, and I wanted to get my strength up before then.'

'Ooh, takes strength to face him, does it?' I asked, covering up the sudden shock of coming head-on to one of his lies, with a phoney bit of joking. Paolo had said he'd be in London on Saturday.

Kim managed a grin.

'Sort of. I've brought my sewing round. . . But if you're going out. . .?'

'It can wait. Nothing important,' I lied, putting my mascara wand back into the bottle, and screwing the top on tightly. I couldn't tell Kim that I was just off to meet her boyfriend, could I?

She looked pale and strained and awkward.

'Tony? Were you off to meet him?' she asked.

I shook my head.

'Still off, for the moment?' she asked.

'It'll come back on, whenever I say the word,' I said, with a flash of anger at yet another pitying comment. But Kim didn't seem to notice the anger.

'Good. . .' she murmured, plonking herself awkwardly on my bed. 'Am I interrupting you? Sure? Look, tell me to go as soon as you've got to go out. This sewing's just an excuse, Jo. I. . . I've got to talk to you. . .'

I held my breath, and crossed my fingers. She looked worried. Very worried. And uneasy. She left the carrier bag and the records on my bed, and went to fiddle among my paperbacks on the other side of the room, standing with her back to me.

'It's about Paolo. . .'

I tensed. It was a good job she couldn't see me. Had she found out?

'Sort of. . . And I've got to ask you a personal question, Jo, a really personal question, but you're the only person I can ask. . . How far've you been with Tony?'

I almost choked. I'd been expecting a bombshell, but not that kind of bombshell from Kim.

'It's none of your damn business!' I spluttered. 'Hell, Kim! If you want to start comparing notes about your love-life you've come to the wrong place. Go and ask Sue Fraser, if you want an answer to that sort of question – she's the one who thinks it's clever to brag about it!'

'Jo. . .' Kim sobbed, turning towards me and coming to sit on the edge of the bed, close to me.

'I'm sorry. I'm not used to all this, and the question came out wrong. You're my only real friend. None of the others could give me the sort of advice I need. I reckon I'm going out of my mind worrying about it.'

'About what exactly?' I asked, carefully, trying to calm myself down.

'Boys. Men. Guys. Them! What do they want, Jo? What're you supposed to do? You know, you hear people saying that boys want only one thing. Sue Fraser's always saying that. Is it true? Do you *have* to? Do they expect it? How far do you have to go. . .?'

Tears were streaming down her face. I hadn't seen her in this state since Carl's accident. But this time there was an awful sick feeling in the pit of my stomach as well as the sympathy I felt for her. The sick feeling had something to do with Paolo, and the fact that I was putting two and two together, slowly. . .

'I don't know, Kim. I honestly don't know. See, although I've been going out with Tony for years, the subject's never come up. It's not that kind of love. It's always been relaxed, y'know, like mates. It's not like that with you and Paolo, though, is it?'

I knew the answer to that one before she spoke. I knew the way Paolo made me feel, almost as if I was losing control. He'd made me believe that I was special, that the feeling was something special, that it had never happened to him, either. And, all the time, he'd probably said the same thing to Kim.

'It's not like you and Tony. No,' Kim sniffed, dragging a crumpled tissue out of her pocket. 'Paolo's older. Well, I've always made out that I was getting really sophisticated, and that it's dead good between us. It is, Jo. The things he says, and the things he does – I can't believe it's happening to me... But he's getting bad tempered with me now, 'cos I keep saying no. I can't bear to lose him!'

'Aw, Kim...' I said, my own eyes filling with tears.

'And don't say it won't happen, Jo! It will. He says so. He says if I don't want him, there's others who do. I'm seeing him tomorrow night, and I don't want to go through the same old scene again. I feel as if I'm being blackmailed by him, just because I love him!'

'You are,' I said quietly.

It was all becoming very clear. 'Just a little longer,' Paolo had said to me. He needed more time to make Kim do what he wanted. And he was using me to work it all. He had me standing in the background to run to if Kim refused him. And meanwhile he was using this threat of there being others who'd be willing to take him away from Kim. There was only one other. Me. Muggins. The idiot who'd believed every sincere lie he'd told me.

I glanced at the clock. It was quarter past seven. I was already quarter of an hour late for my date with him. Well, he could wait all night. Me on Friday, Kim on Saturday, him grinning away to himself that he'd come between us so successfully that we wouldn't share our secret problems... He was right in one thing. I wasn't about to tell Kim that I'd got tied up with him, too. It hurt too much.

But would Paolo tell? I didn't know, now, whether I could trust him at all. If Kim refused him, would he get back at her by telling her about us? I wouldn't put it past him, not now that I was getting the message, loud and clear, about what he was really like.

I could get myself off the hook, though, by telling Kim to play along with him, and agree to what he wanted. That would keep him quiet, for both of us. . .

'Don't let yourself be pushed,' I said, taking a deep breath. 'You've got to tell him where to get off, Kim!'

'But if he leaves me. . .?' she asked tearfully.

'It's a risk you'll have to take. Surely it's better than getting yourself in this state? Stand up to him,' I told her.

'I suppose you're right. I just wish I knew for definite whether this is what being in love's supposed to be all about. I can't take much more of it,' she sighed.

I was trembling all over. It was half-past seven. By now Paolo would have given up. By now he'd be furious with me. I'd got myself into a right old mess with everyone. Kim looked dreadful. I felt dreadful. No guy was surely worth all this.

'Get your coat on,' I said, out of the blue.

'What. . . what for?' she stammered.

'Everyone's going to Boogy's tonight. They've all been talking about it. Let's get down there, and have a night out, and forget all this.'

'I. . . I'm not really dressed for it. . .' Kim argued.

I marched over to my wardrobe and flung the doors open. There wasn't much to rave about in there, just a few summer dresses, and a couple of skirts and tops.

'Here,' I grinned, throwing my silky blue skimmy dress at Kim. 'Crawl into that. It'll suit you. Come on. We'll get you off with Mad Jack!'

'Haven't I got enough problems?' she giggled.

But at least it was a giggle. It was better than the tears. Tonight I was going to dance Paolo out of my system, and make Kim do the same.

Tomorrow, there'd be a lot to think about, and a lot to do. Tonight, I wasn't ready to face anything except music.

'Can I borrow your make-up?' Kim asked, sliding into the blue dress. She looked fantastic in it. I hugged her. She grinned.

'You haven't half cheered me up, Jo,' she said.

That's the price I had to pay for being a two-faced two-timing cheat.

There was just one little arrangement I had to make. While Kim was in the bathroom, I scribbled the note,

Dear Tony. I must see you tomorrow, Saturday, if you can manage it. I've got a lot to tell you. Please ring me and tell me where and when. Love, Joanne.

I'd drop it off at his college room on my way to Boogy's.

Chapter 12

As usual, we had to wait in a queue outside Boogy's. It was always like that, whether the club was full or not, always the queue, always quarter of an hour or so of shivering on the pavement and being bumped and jostled by the people milling around High Street, before Mad Jack finally gave the nod that allowed us in, a few at a time.

Ellen said once that the queue was only kept waiting so that passers-by could see it and think that Boogy's had to be the rock centre of the Universe to be attracting such a lot of people. She said she got goosepimples just being a standing advert for Boogy's.

She was probably right. Because when we finally got Mad Jack's nod, that night, and were let in, there were only about seventy or eighty people in there, and most of them were girls. Friday was free entrance for girls night, and hen-party night, but the hen-parties usually arrived at about nine, and any boys who were turning up arrived even later in big gangs, and had to have their pockets searched for cans of beer.

Seventy or eighty people wasn't exactly the sort of crowd to set the place throbbing, or even humming. When it wasn't bursting at the seams, the full effect of the grottiness of Boogy's really hit you.

Kim sighed as we came out of the cloakroom.

'I used to like this disco. I used to think that coming here was really living!'

'Me, too,' I groaned.

'Paolo ruined it for me, you know. He's ruined a lot of things, sort of before I really got to enjoy them properly.'

I gave her a quick nudge.

'You're not supposed to mention his name, tonight, remember?'

'Sorry. I forgot. We're going to have a great night out, aren't we?'

'Paint the town red,' I agreed, sarkily.

'Boogy on down!' she giggled.

'Right down,' I laughed.

Marie and Ellen were standing at the bar, looking as lost as we felt. I tapped Ellen on the shoulder and she turned and goggled at us.

'What're you two doing here? And what're you doing, Kim Saunders, disguised as Jo? Isn't that your dress, Jo? Anyway, I thought you were ill with a virus. Skiving off school, were you?' she asked Kim.

'Wouldn't you, if you got the chance?' Kim smiled.

That seemed to surprise Ellen, too. It was a long time since Kim had been friendly, ages since she'd had a bit of confidence to backchat with Ellen, weeks since she'd been anything but moody.

'The virus doesn't seem to've done you much harm! Why don't you pass it on to Jo?' Ellen asked.

Marie was busy chatting up the barman, Colin, who wasn't too bad if you were really desperate, but had cross-eyes and never got any of our jokes.

She gave up on him, and came over to us, to a table we'd found right at the edge of the dance floor.

Only the freaks were dancing, the odd few guys who came to Boogy's every night and danced on their own, doing all this body-popping and practising acrobatics. One of them was pretty good, a West Indian kid called Leon. The others were pathetic.

'Look at him. Thinks he's great. Looks like a reject from the teddy-bear factory,' Ellen said glumly, pointing out this fat guy with short rubbery legs and long arms who was getting turned on by his own reflection in the grubby mirrors lining the walls.

'I've decided, El,' Marie said thoughtfully, 'that I was made for better things than this. The art college was fantastic, wasn't it?'

Ellen shot her a warning look.

'OK, OK, I know I'm not supposed to mention it in front of Jo. I know we're all supposed to be careful what we say, but you don't mind, do you, Jo? It's just that if you and Tony finish, this'll be the story of our life, for ever and ever, stuck in Boogy's with cobwebs coming out of our ears, eyeing up guys like that! Not a patch on those art students. . .' she complained.

'Sorry. . .' I muttered.

'Why don't we all dance?' Kim asked.

Marie gawped.

'Us four? Out there?' she winced.

'Why not? Better than sitting here feeling sorry for ourselves,' she said.

She looked as if she'd come out from a long dark tunnel, as if she'd made her mind up about something.

Ellen prodded me as we all got up to dance.

'What've you been saying to Kim? What's happening? She's almost human tonight.'

'Nothing to do with me. Maybe she was human underneath all along,' I suggested.

'Where's this hunky boyfriend of hers, tonight, anyway?' she whispered.

Standing in a car-park, I thought to myself. The thought stabbed at me, painfully.

'Who cares?' I grinned.

The disco was beginning to hot up. Some gangs of older girls came in, giggling and yelling, to sit at the reserved tables up near the DJ. The hen-parties. Some of them staggered on to the dance floor, and started doing the knees-up, and the can-can to the disco records, and screaming cheeky comments at each other.

'That's Verna Fisher. She only left school two years ago. She's getting married tomorrow afternoon at All Saints,' Marie said enviously, rolling around with the beat.

'Marie! Don't you think of anything else?' Ellen groaned.

'Yeah. Food. Bags of crisps. Squodgy cake. Chips. Fish fingers and tomato ketchup. Swiss roll and ice cream,' she drooled. 'Until tomorrow. Tomorrow I'm going on a diet,'

'Not again!' I giggled. 'What for?'

''Cos of you and Kim. Just look at you two. All slim and sexy. That's how you nab the sexy fellas. Me, I just try hard. You two don't even need to try. Hairdressers and art students. I should be so lucky. The nearest I got was Norm. . .'

'I'm getting married in the morning,' Verna Fisher sang, drunkenly, colliding with us as she can-canned with her mates.

'The DJ gives them all a free garter, and a free bottle of champagne,' Marie went on, looking sadder than ever. 'I'd have to put my garter round my wrist. My legs're that fat!'

'Smile,' Ellen hissed. 'Here comes a guy who looks as if he likes fat legs!'

Marie smiled from ear to ear, just in time. Gary from the record shop grabbed her hand, and took her over to the other side of the dance floor.

'One down. Three to go!' Ellen grinned, just before she was caught and hauled off by the reject from the teddy-bear factory. She threw us a despairing look over her shoulder.

'They're OK, really, Marie and Ellen,' Kim said, thoughtfully. 'I always thought Ellen was dead snotty, and Marie was stupid, but they're a good laugh.'

'Yeah,' I agreed, just as I was grabbed round the waist.

Verna Fisher's crowd had started a conga. I pulled Kim into it, too, and we weaved round the room, falling over the other dancers, going in and out of the cloakroom, singing to the record on the way. It was like a madhouse. Verna tried to lead us round the back of the bar and Mad Jack had to step in to block the way. The conga collapsed like dominos, as the DJ announced;

'Who's getting married tomorrow?'

Verna jumped up, dusted herself down, and was

half-carried up to the stage, where she was presented with her garter, and a big kiss from Maurice the DJ who looked like an owl with all its feathers plucked out.

'Do your party piece, then,' Maurice told her.

'Here?' she giggled.

'Give us a song,' he suggested.

So we all had to block our ears up, and boo and whistle as she gathered some of her mates on stage for an ear-splitting version of 'Viva Espana' because she was going to Spain for her honeymoon. Kim whistled and booed too, and laughed at Verna's attempts to dance with Maurice.

'I haven't laughed so much for ages!' she said, holding her stomach. 'Paolo's really po-faced, you know. Dead serious and intense all the time. It's nice, but it can get a bit too important. I hadn't realized what I was missing!'

'No. . .' I murmured.

But Kim had always been a kind of outsider with our mob, standing on the sidelines, too shy, too devastated by Carl's death, to join in with the good times and the silliness. For her, all this was an eye-opener. She'd sneered at it before she'd really been a part of it.

For me, it was different. I'd always been in the centre of things. Paolo had knocked me completely off-balance. Falling in love with him had spoiled the laughs, and put all this gnawing guilt in its place. I was the one who felt uneasy now. And perhaps I'd never fit in again, not after I'd done what I had to do this weekend.

Kim and I went to buy ourselves some cokes. Ellen joined us.

'Heard about the party tomorrow night? Angie's? You coming, Jo?' she asked.

'Got to see someone tomorrow. Tony, as a matter of fact,' I muttered.

'Oh?' she asked, doing her eyebrow raising stunt. I didn't elaborate. She didn't push it.

'What about you, Kim?' she asked, unexpectedly.

'Paolo,' Kim blushed.

'Say no more!' Ellen grinned.

'But. . . I might show up. It depends,' Kim added.

'Oh!' Ellen said again, looking even more surprised.

Marie trundled up.

'Last bus time,' she sighed. 'Still, he says he'll see me at Angie's. Is Sue Fraser coming?'

'Don't know. Jo isn't. But Kim might!' Ellen told her.

'I can kiss Jack bye-bye if Kim's there. And Sue Fraser'll nick Golden boy Gary. Maybe I'll be slim and beautiful tomorrow night, though,' Marie said, hopefully.

'You're OK as you are, Marie!' Kim giggled, linking arms with her, as we walked across to the cloakroom.

I couldn't make out what she'd decided to say to Paolo. But whatever it was, it seemed to have put new life into her. Perhaps talking to me had helped. That made me feel worse than ever.

The three of them joked and giggled on the bus. I joined in when I could. I'd really enjoyed the evening.

I'd enjoyed the badminton game on Wednesday. I'd enjoyed the Fun Swim last Sunday. But always there was the deep-down despair that I couldn't clear.

I stared out of the grimy bus windows, at the lights of town, and the reflection of Kim's laughing face. It took me back to that time I'd been driven by Paolo up the North Alton road towards the Anglers' Arms. Tears misted my eyes. I sniffed them away. If only that could have been a dream, good or bad, that I'd woken from now. If only I could step back in time, a fortnight or so, and take a deep breath and start again. Would I do things any differently, though?

Probably not. I was that much of an idiot.

Tony's message was waiting for me when I got home. He'd phoned, and Mum had written down what he'd said, that he'd meet me outside Hamburger Heaven at half-past-seven tomorrow night, and that we could go on from there.

But there was nowhere to go on to. I crumpled the note in my hand. I had to face the fact that my romance with Tony was over. And my romance with Paolo. And as for my friendship with Kim, that would be over as soon as she knew what I'd been up to behind her back. I didn't blame her. If I had a friend like me, I'd want to see her heartbroken and lonely, too.

But, being me, I didn't know whether I could face it.

Chapter 13

Most of Saturday I hung round the house, completely on edge, wondering whether I ought to go round to Kim's and tell her everything, wondering whether I ought to go round to the salon and yell at Paolo.

I couldn't do either. There was only one person I really wanted to see, and to talk to. For as long as I'd been half grown up, Tony had been there, to talk to, or to write to. My letters to him had been like diaries and problem page requests. He listened so well, even when he pretended to watch the sea, or examine a pebble in his hands. His ears and mind were always tuned in to my voice.

Paolo had been tuned in to himself. I hadn't seen that at the time, because he'd carried me along with believing that I was like him. He'd repeated over and over again how well we understood each other. No way. I'd never understand him, the way he'd played Kim and me against each other just so he could get what he wanted. And yet he'd made me love him. And whenever I thought of him there was that electric tingle, that trembly feeling in my knees, that made me sit down and cry.

At half-past-six, I was ready to meet Tony. I couldn't stay in the house a minute longer, getting under Mum's feet, having her ask me pointless questions like 'What's got into you?' and 'Don't you think you ought to pull yourself together?'

So I walked slowly into town, taking the path I'd

often taken with Kim when we used to go window-shopping round the centre on Saturday mornings.

I walked up to the end of our road, through the park gates and across the playing fields. There was a gang of boys on the football pitch, all wearing City scarves, kicking someone's rolled-up anorak between them. One of the lads waved to me. It was Ellen's Lee, grinning from ear to ear. City had won four-nil at home that afternoon, and it looked as if that was what he was celebrating. I waved back, and headed for the river path.

The park gates. . . Paolo had parked the car there and kissed me on the night I'd told my first lie and opted out of Mandy's party.

The river path was where I'd asked him to walk with me, on Wednesday, when I'd arranged to play badminton, and hadn't got much time.

The path twisted through the trees edging the park, and led out to a bridge and a gate into the car-park, our car-park, our place for those secret stolen meetings. I'd thought they were so romantic. I'd seen the whole thing through a haze of love like the haze over these slow September evenings. Really it had been a bit sordid and scruffy, all that hiding, meeting in car-parks, driving away from the prying eyes that could probably see through it all.

But still I couldn't stop crying.

On the corner of Church Street, I wiped my eyes on the cuff of my ski-coat, fuzzed my hair out, and quickened my step, just in case any of my mates were in the Hamburger Heaven, sitting at the stools against the window, and watching to see who they could see.

But it was only quarter-past-seven when I arrived, too early for any of my crowd to come into the café before Angie's party. There were only a couple of first years, kids I'd seen in the corridors and at assembly, sharing cokes with two boys in Scout uniforms, and a few courting couples passing the time until the start of the big film at the ABC opposite.

I ordered a coke and sat near the back facing the window, and waited, and tried not to think of what I was going to say. The words would come, and they'd be all wrong, but Tony would sort them out somehow.

I didn't have long to wait. I saw him crossing the road by the traffic lights, peering through the windows, and then throwing open the door to have a better look inside. I waved. He smiled. It was as if the door had opened to let the sun shine through.

He collected a coke, and came over to me, all eager, all enthusiastic, like the little kid he used to be.

'Hi, Jo! Great to see you,' he grinned, bending down to touch my hair and kiss my cheek. 'Got it all sorted out then?'

'Not really. . .' I murmured, raising my eyes to his.

He looked stunned for a minute, and then smiled again, but this time his smile wasn't very real.

'What's happened?' he asked.

'I just wanted to talk to you,' I said, quietly. 'Kim came round last night.'

'Oh yeah?'

'To tell me all about this Paolo, and to ask my advice. That's funny, isn't it? You know what she asked me? She wanted to know what fellas want, y'know, when they're supposed to be in love. She asked me because she thought I'd know how you felt about things. But I never got round to asking you, did I? The question never came up.'

Tony sighed, brushed the floppy hair from his eyes with his fingers, and looked at me out of the corner of his eye.

'So that's the kind of guy he is!' he murmured. 'I thought so. I've met guys like that!'

'What's that supposed to mean?' I asked.

'Kim wanted to know what guys want? They want the same things as girls. Friendship, love, a sense of humour, things to share. That's what they want. Or at least, that's what I've always wanted. I've always wanted someone I could talk to, about things that mattered to me. But it sounds as if Kim's guy was trying to tell her that he wanted a lot more than that.'

I nodded.

'Like I said, I thought that might be the problem. It sounded to me as if she was showing off about him, and you only do that if you're covering up, if things aren't quite right.'

'I showed off about you!' I argued.

'So badly that you lost your mates?' he asked.

'No.'

'Right. So Kim's being pushed. What's she going to do about it?'

I shrugged. 'Don't know. I told her to stand up for herself.'

'Hmm. Think she will?' he asked.

'I reckon so. I've been thinking about it all day, and she seemed so much better after she'd got it all off her chest, that she'll probably have the confidence to tell him where to get off,' I said.

'Good. She's done the best thing. She's come right out and told you about it. That always helps,' he smiled.

'Does it?' I asked.

'Sharing secrets sorts them out. . . That guy of hers sounds a real smoothie. Fancy picking on someone like Kim!' he said.

'And. . . there's more. . .' I stammered. I held on tightly to my glass of coke. It was starting to tremble in my hand. And the tears were coming from nowhere. I couldn't stop them. I couldn't look at Tony. I knew his eyes too well. I knew that colour, that blue-green misty colour, and the look that said 'I'll listen' and I didn't want to change all that, and bring the clouds across. . . 'There's me, too, Tony.'

He listened. There was a tension in him that I'd never sensed before as I struggled to find the words, as if I were on the other side of a piece of steamed-up glass, and he was waiting for the glass to break.

I told him the whole story, right from that silly phone-call that Marie encouraged me to make for the hairdressing appointment. I told him about each secret meeting, the quiet of that restaurant, the shimmer of the river outside the window of the pub, the blue lights that shone on the tiny dance floor in the Plaisir disco. I told him why I hadn't been at home to meet him on the day he arrived, and why I hadn't read his letter.

And I told him why Paolo had wanted me, all along, to be someone to fall back on, and to blackmail Kim with. And I told him I was sorry, sorrier than I'd ever been about anything. I told him I knew that didn't help.

'Did you love him?' he asked, very quietly.

'I don't know, Tony! I honestly don't know. I know what a slimy character he is, and I know he's used me, and I don't want to see him again. But. . .'

His fingertips touched mine, briefly. I looked up. There were tears in his eyes, too.

'It's over between us, isn't it, Jo?' he asked.

It was what I didn't want to say, but knew all along. It had to be over. I'd seen something else, and although the anger and bitterness of what the something else had done to me would never go away, nor would the memories. Tony had never made the whole world tilt for me, as Paolo had done. Tony's caring had been real. Paolo, though, had shaken me right through, for the moment.

The Hamburger Heaven was filling up. The door banged open and closed, letting in the cold wind. There was laughter from the seats by the windows and someone yelled,

'OK, so none of us've been invited. We'll gatecrash. My ex-girlfriend'll be there. She'll let us in. Just ask for Ellen. . .'

'Right. So we say Lee sent us?' another voice roared.

'Yeah, but I'll go first. I'll talk her round. Give me five minutes, then you lot turn up and. . . no football! Remember? No talking about City tonight. They don't like football. . .'

'I think it's over,' I whispered,

'I think it *is* because I came down here. I think I made you feel trapped. It was different in Brighton, just the summers, something to look forward to all year. . . And we got stuck in being the boy and girl next door, didn't we? Brother and sister. Not very exciting,' Tony said, huskily.

'I wanted you to come. . .' I sobbed. 'And then, when you did, it'd all gone wrong. Everything was different.'

'I suppose it'll stay different?' he asked.

I nodded.

'What're you going to do now?'

'I'll have to find a way to tell Kim. Maybe he's already told her. She's seeing him tonight. And then, I suppose, I'll just have to get over it,' I sniffed.

'If you need a shoulder to cry on. . .' Tony murmured, taking one of my hands in both of his.

'How can I? How can I use you, Tony? I can't treat you like that. It's best just to finish. Marie said all the art college girls were eyeing you up. . .'

He shrugged, and smiled weakly.

'Bet you've already got someone lined up,' I said, joking pathetically.

'Maybe I have,' he grinned, without a trace of that twinkle in his eye that always appeared with one of his grins.

'I knew it! Well. . . I'll send you a Christmas card,' I said, standing.

'And I'll send you a postcard from Brighton,' he said.

We walked out together, through the crush of people waiting at the take-away counter. Saturday

117

night. The streets were crowded with couples arm in arm, hand in hand, sharing secret smiles, jokes, whispers, promises. My eyes were lost behind the tears, but there was still so much love to see.

We eased through the crowds outside the ABC, and the queue at Boogy's. We walked through Cathedral Close, and past the line of gleaming cars parked outside the Plaisir disco. We walked together all the way to the art college without saying another word.

'Well. . . I'd better go in. Sean and Lewis're waiting for us. . . me. . . by the bar in the disco. Take care, Joanne. . .' he murmured.

'Will. . . will you settle in OK. . . now?' I asked.

'I'm already settled. Loads of work to do. You should see the first year assignments! Good job this is only a foundation year. I can move on to another college where the work's a bit easier, next summer,' he said.

'Can you do that? Will you do that? Move on?' I breathed.

'Nearly everyone does. It's expected. You go to another college to do your three years of art training in your speciality – sculpture, silversmithing, fine art – that's painting – graphics, illustration. I'll probably move on.'

'Oh,' I said.

'We'll probably bump into each other, some time,' he stammered.

'Yeah,' I said.

''Bye, Jo,' he croaked.

''Bye, Tony,' I whispered.

He turned and walked up the steps. Moving on.

His shoulders were hunched, and his hands clenched inside the pockets of his jacket. He didn't look like my Tony at all.

And I probably didn't look like his Joanne. I couldn't remember his Joanne crying like this before, right in the street, not caring who saw her, crying as if her heart was breaking.

It *was* breaking. He'd forgotten to ask me whether I still loved him, and the answer was the same answer I'd given him on the beach, this summer, when he'd shown me the letter and asked me if I wanted him around. It was the same answer I'd given him when he asked me years ago if I was going to be his girl.

But he'd only asked me if I still loved Paolo. He should've asked me if I loved him. And I'd've said, without needing to think 'Yes, Tony. Yes, yes, yes. I love you. I'll always love you.'

And maybe that little voice inside me would've whispered, so that only I could hear, 'But I don't deserve you, so I'll have to let you go.'

So I sat on the low wall in front of the cathedral, and cried my heart out in the darkness.

Chapter 14

Mum guessed, of course, about Tony and me. She guessed as soon as I came in on Saturday night, with my eyes all red-rimmed and my nose all sniffy. But she said nothing then. She just made me a cup of coffee, and I took that into my room, away from the stupid noise of the telly, and away from all the questions.

On Sunday morning, though, she asked me right out, and I had to tell her that we'd finished.

'Any reason?' she asked.

'Oh, you know, just this and that. It's difficult going steady, and keeping your mates, and Tony thought that he was getting in the way a bit.'

I managed to get that out. Then I had to go and lock myself in the bathroom, because the real reason for the break-up kept coming up on me in great waves of nausea. All I wanted to do was to hide and cry, and never see Kim again, and never have to tell her the truth about what I'd done to her and to Tony. If I couldn't face it, she wouldn't be able to, either.

But I wasn't going to be spared that. I'd just finished dunking my face in cold water and drying off the tears, and dragged myself downstairs again, when there was a ring of a bike bell in our front path. I hadn't heard that sound for ages. For a moment, I thought it was one of next door's little kids, and then I saw Marie and Kim wobbling up to our back door on their bikes.

Kim knocked on the door, and opened it, and breezed in.

'C'mon. Rise and shine. Look at that blue sky! Get your old bike out of the garage, Jo. We're off on a bike ride!'

'I . . . I don't think . . . ' I stammered.

'It'll do you good, Joanne,' Mum interrupted, coming up behind me, and putting her arm round my shoulders. I could just about see her, out of the corner of my eye, giving Kim a warning glance that said, 'Watch out for Joanne. She's feeling very fragile this morning.' Kim was looking puzzled, when Marie trotted in, wearing a bright yellow tracksuit with red bands along the arms and across the chest, and the number 89 on the front.

'Very sporty!' Mum grinned appreciatively. 'What does the number mean?'

'I got it in the sales, so I didn't ask. But I know now. It's how old I feel when I try to pedal that bike,' Marie groaned. 'Something needs oiling. My left knee, I think!'

Kim giggled.

'It's Marie's diet. She came round to our house at the crack of dawn, ate all the toast Mum'd made me for breakfast, and then said she had to go on a bike ride to work the calories off,' she explained.

'I haven't worked them off yet. They've just worked their way down to my knees. Coming, Jo? Get a move on before I change my mind. I need you for the "before and after" picture. You and Kim're what I'm going to look like after this diet. I'm serious!'

'Where's Ellen?' I asked, pulling a sweat-shirt over my t-shirt. There was no arguing with them, and anyway, I had to talk to Kim some time. By the look of her, the cares of the world had suddenly been lifted from her shoulders. Paolo obviously hadn't told her about us. It was down to me, however painful that was going to be.

'She's back with Lee,' Marie sighed. 'Would you believe it? He says if City win the relegation battle, he'll turn over a new leaf and never bother about soccer again. It's a stupid deal. But Ellen looks happy enough about it.'

'They were all over each other at Angie's party last night,' Kim said, as I scrabbled through the coal-shed and into the garage for my rusty old heap of a bike.

I stopped, grabbing the saddle in one dusty hand.

'You went? To Angie's party?' I breathed.

'Yeah. Tell you about it all later,' she whispered.

'What about Paolo?' I asked.

She grinned and tossed her fine glossy hair out of her eyes.

'Tell you about that, too!' she bubbled.

'What's keeping you two?' Marie yelled.

'Coming,' I shouted.

I wheeled the bike down the drive, blowing the dust off the saddle at the same time.

'We'll ride down the river path, and make for North Alton,' Marie suggested, turning left out of our front gate.

'No!' I said, and then added, quickly. 'Let's ride down the London Road to the old airfield. There's a

Sunday Market on. We can look round for cheap clothes!'

'Right. And have hot-dogs to cheer us up!' Marie drooled, changing direction and pedalling like mad.

'Marie! No hot-dogs. Remember the diet,' Kim reminded her.

'Don't Guardian Angels take Sundays off?' Marie asked her pleadingly.

'No. This Guardian Angel's going to make sure you turn into a skinny beanpole by Christmas,' Kim giggled.

'I don't know whether I'd rather be thin or sin!' Marie laughed.

And then we had to go like the wind to get enough speed to climb Forest Hill.

My legs creaked. I was getting too old for this kind of thing, especially in the shaky state I was in. The wind blew my hair back and scrubbed my cheeks until they glowed. It was like all those walks I'd taken with Tony across windswept beaches, when we'd run hand in hand towards the waves, that shiny exhilarating feeling of being alive to everything. Except that, just now, although my skin tingled, I felt dead inside.

From the top of Forest Hill, I looked over my shoulder, and looked at the city lying in the hollow. The spire of the cathedral, and the gaunt tower of the art college stood next to each other against the pale skyline, and the river circled them like a shiny ribbon.

Up here, the ground levelled out, and pedalling was easier. We settled down riding two abreast, and one behind, and then in single file as cars came roaring past. Funnily enough, it was Kim and Marie who rode next to each other. I was the one at the back, listening to their shaky laughter, but locked in my own black dreamworld.

There was a stream of cars, now, travelling at snail's pace up to the entrance of the old airfield. We climbed off our bikes, and propped them against the fence, and walked through the muddy gateway, down to the parked caravans and lorries and the ramshackle stalls.

'I've not brought any money with me!' Marie moaned, as the smell of hot-dogs and onions, candyfloss and doughnuts wafted towards us from the vans.

'That settles the hot-dog argument, then!' Kim said.

'If I kneel down in my new yellow track suit, in the mud, and beg you to lend me fifty pence, Kim?'

'No chance!'

'Jo?'

'Well. . .?'

'Don't weaken, Jo. Don't let her blackmail you!' Kim grinned.

Blackmail. The word shuddered through me. It was the word I'd used for what Paolo had done to her. I think she realized, too. She put her arm round my shoulders.

'What d'you reckon? Do we give in to these heart-rending pleas, and let her eat herself fat again?' Kim asked me, all pretend serious.

I tried to join in. 'Well, there's the bike ride home. That should burn off the onions,' I said.

'And then Sunday lunch?' Kim asked.

'I'm not eating any! Cabbage and one roast spud only, and a very thin slice of meat, and just a splodge of gravy. And I told Mum, only a very small piece of apple pie afterwards. Surely there's room for a hot-dog? And I promise to jog round the park this afternoon!' Marie begged.

'Who could refuse her!' I laughed. 'Here. Fifty pence. And remember, you owe me a favour after this.'

'Thanks, Jo! You're a pal!' Marie grinned, excitedly, taking the fifty pence piece, and running across to join the queue at the hot-dog stand. Kim and I wandered down towards the stalls.

'I finished with Paolo,' Kim announced, quietly, happily.

'You didn't! How? What did he say?' I breathed.

'Nothing. I didn't give him a chance. He can be a bit too persuasive when you're face to face with him. One glance from those sultry Italian eyes, Jo, and I was a goner, every time. So I wrote him a note, and took it round to reception at the salon, and walked out without seeing him. Chicken, eh?'

'No. Not chicken at all. It must've taken a lot of nerve for you to finish with him. I couldn't. . .' I started to say, and then realized what I was saying and changed tack suddenly, hoping she wouldn't notice '. . .er. . . I couldn't've found the courage to finish with him, if I'd been in your place. What did you say in the letter?'

'Oh, the usual stuff, I suppose. I said it was all getting a bit too heavy for me, and that I'd decided that I was better off not seeing him at all. I said he was free to go off with all those thousands of other girls now. . . But I'm a bit sorry, in a way,' she sighed. 'I don't know whether it's him I'll miss, or all the flash places he took me to. I was riding high for a while, with him, you know. Maybe it did me some good. It got me over being so painfully shy. A guy like Paolo can make you feel on top of the world. The rat!'

She laughed, without any bitterness at all. I could feel my throat tightening. Any time now, any time now I was going to burst into tears again, and after the tears, the confessions. And after that. . . what?

'And what about you and Tony? From the look your mum gave me. . . is that all finished,' she went on, saving me from the confession, but not from the tears.

'Yes. . .' I sniffed. 'Last night.'

'But why, Jo? I don't want to nose in, not when you're all upset, but what went wrong? You and Tony looked as if you were teamed up for good.'

'Here's Marie. I'll tell you when we get back,' I said, wiping my eyes, hurriedly on the back of my hand. 'I've got to tell you, anyway.'

Marie trundled up like a bright yellow balloon, smiling and chewing at the same time. Kim was still staring at me, looking bewildered. Marie looked at each of us in turn.

'Bad news?' she asked, fading the smile.

'Just Tony and me,' I sniffed.

She nodded, sadly, and went on eating her hot-dog. That was the great thing about Marie. For someone with non-stop chatter, there were times when she knew how to keep her mouth closed. I liked her. And now that Kim was straightened out, and happy and relaxed, we could all have been great mates. Not once I broke the news to Kim, though. Not after that. There're some things that cut right across even the closest friendships.

For an hour we walked round the market, holding up t-shirts against each other, checking out the faults in the sub-standard jeans, rifling through the tubs of bikinis at cut prices with Marie moaning all the time that she shouldn't have eaten the hot-dog, and Kim joking with her and me thinking that there was no point in looking for new clothes just at the moment.

Then we cycled off home, Marie clutching the pop poster that Kim had lent her the money for. It was easier going down Forest Hill than coming up. Kim, crazily, took her feet off the pedals and stretched them out in front of her as she freewheeled down. She was in the sort of careless silly mood to do that kind of thing. Marie kept whooping. Kim was singing. I followed, my feet on the pedals, both my hands on the brakes.

We left Marie at her house, and cycled round to Kim's.

'Come and sit on the wall for a minute,' she said. 'I'd ask you in, but you know what my mum's like about her precious carpets, and Dad worked overtime last night so he's in bed. Come back Paolo, and take me away from all this!' She laughed, despairingly. 'Sunday lunch in ten minutes, then Gran's all afternoon, then church. Roll on Monday morning and school! Hey, guess what?. . . I was talking to Jack for ages, last night. He's quite nice when you get to know him. With a bit of luck. . .'

She glanced at me, and sighed.

'Come on, Jo. What is it you've got to tell me? I'm just filling in time, rabbiting on about this. What is it? Don't get upset. Whatever it is, it's not worth getting upset about. Look at me. I was in a terrible state over Paolo, and it just wasn't worth it, so. . .'

'So I'm in a terrible state about Paolo, too,' I said.

It came out in a kind of yell. All wrong. Horribly wrong. I watched Kim's face tighten up, and lose all its colour.

'What're you talking about, Jo?' she asked, nervously.

'Me, and Paolo. I went to see him, to check him out, two or three weeks ago, and it just went on from there. I don't know what to say, Kim. I had to tell you. I can't go on feeling like this. . . And don't look at me like that. Please! I stood him up on Friday night. . .'

'While I was. . . while I was pouring out my heart to you?' she breathed.

'Look, I'm sorry. I was the one he was threatening you with. Last night, he'd've told you about me, and used me to twist your arm. He's no good, Kim. I know that, now.'

'*He's* no good?' she screamed. 'What about you, Jo Farmer? What kind of a mate are you supposed to be? You've just been laughing yourself sick, haven't you, at the big joke on me? I can just hear you, you and Paolo, going on about poor old Kim!'

Three weeks, and you didn't even tell me? Three weeks? There're words for you, you know, except that I wouldn't give you the pleasure of hearing me use them. You're sick. And shut up! I don't want to hear the details. I've heard enough. That's plenty!'

She stumbled and almost fell over her bike in her rush to get away from me and into the house. I could hear her sobs echoing in the passage-way down to her back door.

I'd blown it. But what else did I expect? I'd lost my best mate. It was always on the cards.

Chapter 15

After the tears, and the weeks of guilt, and Kim's final explosion, I just went numb. I felt completely drained, empty of all feeling. I went to lie in my room on Sunday afternoon, and stared at the ceiling for hours, and still there was nothing, and on Monday morning, I went off to school like a mindless robot, early, after a sleepless night.

There was no point waiting for Kim to call. I queued for the early bus, but the driver went right by the stop, waving his hand at me to let me know that it was full.

I just stood there, staring into nothing, listening to

the quiet buzz in my head, a blank kind of buzz like the buzz on an empty television screen. I didn't see Kim.

She came up behind me, and tapped me on the shoulder. I jumped a mile.

'Jo. . .' she murmured. 'I called round for you. I've been thinking. . .'

My throat was all sore and tight. I couldn't say anything at all.

'We've been mates for a long time. You were the only one who stuck with me, all along. And after Carl's accident, you were the one who came round. Everyone else thought it was kinder just to leave me crying on my own. I'm not saying I'm going to forget all this. I don't know how long that'll take. But we've got something in common, haven't we?'

I nodded, blindly.

'That Paolo!' she spat. 'This is what he counted on, all along. He tried to work it so that he'd get between us. D'you see that, Jo?'

I nodded. The bus pulled in at the stop, behind us. Neither of us made the effort to get on it. It pulled away again.

'So, I don't really want him to win. Do you?' she asked.

'Not really,' I croaked.

'If we break up, you and me, it'll be what he wanted. I reckon he's loused me up. But he's really broken you. I mean. . . you and Tony. Is this why you split up with Tony?'

I admitted it. 'I told him. Like I told you. Only I told you both too late.'

'Did he. . . did Paolo try the same thing with you that he did with me?' she asked, suddenly.

'No. I think I was "first reserve",' I said, finding my voice at last. 'I wasn't really in the picture. You were the one he was trying to get to.'

Kim sighed, and smiled awkwardly.

'That shouldn't make me feel better, but I think it does. When you told me yesterday, I just had this awful suspicion that you'd given way. I thought the worst of you. Then when I stopped crying, and started thinking, I worked out that you couldn't've been two-faced enough to react the way you did to me on Friday night if. . . I'm not saying you're not two-faced!' she said, half-jokingly. 'Don't want you to get the wrong impression. . .'

She glanced at her watch.

'We'd better start walking!' she announced. 'It's five to nine!'

We walked. Kim talked. And, slowly I felt reality creeping back into that empty space that used to be my heart. It hurt. Kim was telling me about Paolo, asking me about him. It was obvious that both of us still had this funny confused feeling about him.

But he'd said the same words – all that stuff about understanding, and being two of a kind, and needing us. At the time it had sounded beautiful, part of the sunsets and the bright lights and the purr of that soft music on his stereo system. Now it sounded pathetic, like the rerun of a telly programme you've seen too many times.

'We've got to see him,' Kim said, as we approached the school gates.

'You can. I'm not!' I snapped.

'No, I mean together. Tonight. We've got to go up there, to the salon, and show him that we've sussed him out, and that he's not come between us!' she said.

'Hasn't he?' I asked.

'Well. . . not in the way he thinks. We're speaking, just about. We've got to show him that we're not the idiots he took us for, haven't we?'

'I suppose so,' I muttered.

'So, will you?' she asked.

'What do I say?' I trembled. I wasn't sure whether I could even look at him. I hated him. He'd lost me Tony. And yet, I'd loved him every time he gave me that special look. I didn't know whether I could beat it.

'OK,' I said, for Kim's sake.

'Good. Home time. We'll sort him out, Jo. We'll put a real scare into him. . . Come on now, run past the staffroom. We've got to look as if we've made some effort to get to school!'

We ran. My knees wobbled. They hadn't stopped letting me down since Friday. And now Kim was suggesting this crazy meeting! But maybe she was right. If I could hold out, facing Paolo together might be the jolt he needed to show him that girls weren't as stupid as he seemed to think they were.

The day was full of reminiscences about Angie's party, and everyone was talking about Lee and Ellen. Especially Ellen. She was all starry-eyed again. It made me wonder what love was all about if it could turn off and on like a hot water tap.

Marie was boasting about her success on her diet, and eating biscuits non-stop right through break.

I stood back. The word had got round that Tony and I had really finished this time, but it wasn't the important gossip of the day. After Ellen, Kim was the big news. She was right in there, in the centre of things, giggling with Marie, back-chatting with Ellen, listening open-mouthed as Sue Fraser tried to get into the spotlight with more amazing boasting about what she probably hadn't done.

No one seemed to notice the awkwardness between Kim and me. I suppose they thought that I was too upset about Tony to join in the laughter.

It was strange, being on the outside, watching Kim holding her own. In a way I felt proud, because I was the one who'd always known about the personality that she hid under self-consciousness. But I felt as if she'd never really trust me again. And that upset me more than anything.

At home time, anyone seeing us walking out together would've thought we were still best friends. You'd have to be close to us to realize that the signs of real friendship just weren't there any more. We weren't whispering to each other, or nudging each other, or sharing private jokes. We were stiff and a bit formal, like well-mannered strangers, being careful not to stand too close.

We talked, though. Mostly about Paolo again. Kim had to get it off her chest. Me, I just wanted to forget. I was all raw edges, and self-control, with the tears clamped inside.

'Is that where Paolo took you?' Kim asked, when we passed the Plaisir disco.

'Yeah,' I said.

'He never took me there!' she snapped, revealing, just for a moment, that she hurt, too, not so much about the big betrayal, but about little things that I'd shared with him and she hadn't.

Kim suggested we sat on a bench, outside the Town Hall, where we could keep an eye on Paolo's parked car, and, if we craned our necks, could see everyone coming out of the salon.

We must have sat there for at least three-quarters of an hour. I was shivery with tension and the effort of sitting still. Kim kept saying,

'I can't wait to see his face!'

She'd got it all worked out. As soon as we saw Paolo coming, we'd walk towards his car, so that he'd meet us head on. She was going to say, 'Joanne and I have been having a little talk about you.'

And I was supposed to say, 'I've heard Kim's side of it. Now what've you got to say for yourself?'

He was supposed to squirm, and look deflated and defeated, and start making pathetic excuses, while we stood and grinned. It was the best we could do to make him suffer, just a little, for the agonies he'd put both of us through.

The Town Hall struck quarter to six.

'How much longer?' I asked, hugging myself to try to keep warm, my teeth chattering.

'He's got to come out soon!' Kim sighed, stretching to look at the salon door for the millionth time.

'He's here!' she gasped.

We both saw him. Neither of us moved. He couldn't see us, huddled together on that bench amongst the tired shoppers and people walking home from work. We were too far away.

And anyway, he wasn't looking at us. He was looking at the girl.

She was small and blonde, nestling in the crook of his arm, smiling up at him as if every crinkle round his laughing eyes demanded her loving attention. She reached up, and flicked his hair back with her finger-tips, and giggled as he kissed her nose.

'He's found someone else!' Kim breathed.

'Another idiot,' I murmured, bewildered.

'Is she new, d'you think? Or was she there all along?' Kim asked.

'Does it matter?' I asked.

He eased the girl into his car. I followed every one of his smooth movements, every one of the careful expressions on his lying face, each strutting step he took. That girl had been me. It had been Kim. We were all the same to him.

The car purred away. Inside it Paolo was probably purring, too. We'd left him, and it meant nothing at all to him.

'Well!' Kim snorted. 'So much for showing him up. Fat chance we had. He wouldn't've turned a hair!'

I stood up, shivering all over.

'That's that,' I said, wearily.

I had nothing left. I'd not even managed to get a

bit of my pride back by standing up to Paolo. At least Kim had the satisfaction of knowing she'd finished with him. I didn't even have that.

Kim was muttering angrily under her breath. I couldn't manage anger. Just bewilderment, just a sense of uselessness.

Kim linked my arm.

'Don't look so hopeless, Jo. At least now we know!'

'Right,' I said, trying to smile. Knowing didn't help me much. Nothing helped. Maybe time would, but it was going to take a long long time before either of us could forgive me for the mistakes I'd made and the mess I'd made of everything.

Kim was going swimming with Ellen and Marie, later on. I'd heard them making the arrangements. They probably thought I wouldn't want to go. I didn't think they were deliberately leaving me out. Kim would never tell them what I'd done. I was pretty certain of that, because there'd been too much friendship between us in the past.

And perhaps that closeness would come back, some day. . .

Chapter 16

Almost Christmas. I've made it this far.

Boogy's is bursting at the seams tonight. Even Mad Jack's catching Christmas fever, letting far too many of us in. It's Marie's wink. It works miracles on him.

'Full up, what d'you mean?' she pleaded with him at the door. 'C'mon Jack. You know me! And Ellen, and Kim, and sexy Joanne. We'll not stand on the tables and sing football songs or swing on the Christmas decorations, will we, girls? And anyway, it was my birthday yesterday, and you forgot to buy me a present, so. . .'

He let us in.

Marie's birthdays come in handy. She has about ten a year. Ellen says she had more birthdays than diets, and by rights she ought to be collecting her pension by now, and be slimmed down to a needle. And Marie just laughs and says, 'What, and be as old and sharp as you?'

Mind you, Marie looks pretty good these days, not at all as if she ought to go on a diet or stop having birthdays. She's as plumply happy as ever, just building up, she says, for a big Christmas romance, and tonight's the night she's going to find her dream guy, according to her. She looks like part of the Christmas decorations, in her silver jumpsuit with that red-gold tumble of curls shimmering in the spots of light from the whirling globe up on the ceiling.

But just at the moment, it doesn't look as if she's found the dream guy. She's dancing with Sam, and grinning at me over his shoulder as if to say, 'This isn't the big thing, you know!'

But Sam's improved. Boys do, as they get older. He's taken to wearing clothes that don't look as if his brother's already slept in them, and his skin's clearing, and his hair's growing out of that Scout haircut he used to have. He even found time to stop in the middle of a long boring lecture to me about computer science the other night to say, 'Am I boring you?' Now that's got to be an improvement. Perhaps Marie won't go far wrong with him.

Ellen's dancing next to Marie and Sam. She's wearing long glittery earrings, really dangly ones that hang down to her shoulders. And Lee's dancing opposite her, without his City scarf on. I haven't seen that scarf for ages, come to think of it. And I haven't heard Ellen moaning about the soccer thing. Kim says they'll get engaged soon, maybe in the summer, when Ellen starts her pre-nursing course. But I can't see it. Ellen's the wait-and-see kind. Kim's more the incurable romantic.

She's sitting next to me now, telling me about last Wednesday's badminton match. There's only the two of us at the table. All the other chairs have got bags and coats on. There's Marie's canvas hold-all, with Spike, her good-luck charm, an evil-looking plastic crocodile, poking out of the gap, there's Ellen's neat black leather handbag, that her mum and dad gave her for her seventeenth birthday last week, there's Sam's coat, and Lee's coat, and Jack's denim bomber.

He's over at the bar, buying us some cokes, standing right under the sign that says, 'Happy

Christmas'. Every so often, he turns to smile at Kim, and she grins back. Even when she's supposed to be telling me about the badminton match she can't take her eyes off him.

I think she's really settled, this time. She doesn't. She keeps saying to me, 'I'm not counting on it, Jo.' But she is. I can almost hear it ticking in her heart as she talks, with those shiny eyes sparking, and that bobbed blonde-streaked hair continually pushed behind her ears while she denies that she's in love.

I'm happy for her. I've told her that. But I think she'd rather hear it from Marie or Ellen. Still that old hurt comes up and gets in the way of what we really want to say to each other. It hasn't quite healed.

She's the one, now, who stands between Marie and Ellen at lunchtime, acting as referee, laughing at the jokes and snide comments. I've taken her place.

Usually, I just sit and listen.

And think.

And remember.

And when those moods come on me, those drifting dreamy moods when I cut off from everyone and from everything that's going on around me, I settle back, not in the memories of Paolo's intense kisses, or the good times he showed me.

No. I'm back in Brighton. It's summer. There's a breeze blowing in from the sea, and a blue sky above, and I'm resting easy in Tony's encircling arm, and he's saying, 'You'll get tired of me, one day, Jo,' and I'm saying, 'Never. I'll always love you,' and a seagull cries above us three times, like a warning.

It's Tony's eyes I see, on the odd Saturday night parties when someone smiles down at me and asks me to join in the dancing. And it's Tony's smile I try to smile, just to remind myself that once upon a time, before the world caved in, that smile was only for me.

And sometimes, still, I cry.

And sometimes I read his letters, over and over again, and try to hear his gentle, slightly husky voice saying the words that I read.

I've bought a special Christmas card for him. It's a picture of a snow scene, with one bare lonely tree in the centre. I'll just write, inside, 'Best wishes, Jo,' because I know that all he'll want from me is my best wishes.

I've caught sight of him, once or twice, in the town. But I've always ducked into the nearest doorway. He's been with Lewis, or Shaun, or a crowd of other students, some of them girls, and I just haven't been able to face being introduced to one of those girls, and Tony saying, 'Joanne, this is my girl. . .'

I don't want to know. Once he said 'my girl' and it was me.

'Jo, you've switched off again!' Kim grumbles, nudging me. 'You need switching on by that hunky telly star who turned the Christmas illuminations on!'

'Chance'd be a fine thing!' I laugh.

'Or. . .'

And then she freezes, and stares out into the crush of people on the dance floor, under the tinsel garlands, and the sprigs of plastic mistletoe.

I try to see what she's looking at.

'Oh no. . .!' she breathes.

Then I see him, dancing. Rock'n'roll. The girl's all out of step, falling over his feet and her own, twisting gawkily when he tries to swirl her round. Tony. Who else would make my heart stop? Only him.

'I'm. . .I'm sorry. . .' Kim murmurs, squeezing my arm.

She knows how I feel. I've never had to tell her, exactly, but she's noticed how I rarely dance at parties, how I clam up when the others talk about the guys they fancy, how I can't stop loving him.

The girl has long black hair, and a piece of silver tinsel round her neck. I wonder if he put it there, and whispered, 'Nearly Christmas. . .' and 'I love you. . .'

The music stops. That's typical of Boogy's. Only one turntable, and these embarrassing silences at the end of a session of records, when everyone claps and stamps their feet, and the DJ comes running up the steps from the bar with a ham sandwich in his hands. Typical.

'Not here!' Kim whispers.

Tears are pouring down my face.

'Don't, Jo. It's nearly Christmas. Then it'll be a whole New Year. Please don't cry.'

Jack saunters back with the cokes and kisses her forehead, and she leans up towards the kiss, and I just glimpse a figure walking past us to the next table, a girl with long black hair, who settles next to a red-haired guy and says 'I'm back, love. Why can't he bring a girl of his own to dance with, if he wants to do all that fancy dancing?'

'Hi, Joanne,' Tony murmurs.

I look up the whole length of his long legs, right up past his checked shirt, to the quiet smile on his lips.

'It's been a long time,' he says.

'Yes. . .' I stammer.

Kim's nudging me in wild excitement, but I can't move. It's the look in his eyes. It's still the same. It's Brighton beach. It's Rottingdean. It's Hamburger Heaven. It's the mist and the sea. It's where I want to drown, and it's inviting me in.

The DJ pulls himself together.

'OK, weirdos. Here's one specially for you lot. And a Happy Christmas to you, too!' he screams.

The amplifiers belt out 'Rave on'. Our song.

'Let's show them, Jo!' Tony laughs, pulling at my hand.

I follow him on to the dance floor. He grins at me, runs his finger gently down my cheek, and starts to move to the music. I take my lead from him, going with the beat, timing my movements with his, seeing the faces moving back, the hands clapping, the feet stamping. Marie and Ellen and Kim, Jack and Lee and Sam, they're all there, circled round us, shouting encouragement and approval. The smiles blur into the tinsel glitter and the lights from the tall Christmas tree as I twist round into Tony's arms on the final beat of the music.

And then the applause, just as his lips touch mine.

Pam Lyons
Danny's Girl £1.25

For sixteen-year-old Wendy, life was pretty straightforward. She enjoyed her tomboy existence with her parents and brother Mike on their farm in Norfolk. Then, late one sunny September afternoon, Danny wandered into her life and suddenly Wendy's happy and uncomplicated world is turned upside-down. Unsure of how she should behave or what is expected of her, she allows herself to be carried along in Danny's wake, and when he finds himself in trouble at his exclusive boarding school he is her only ally. Eventually, Wendy's fierce loyalty to the boy she loves leads them both deeper and deeper into trouble . . .

Mary Hooper
Follow that Dream £1.25

Her parents' dream of moving to Cornwall is a nightmare blow for Sally. How could she bear to leave London and be stuck away in the country . . . with no mates, no music, no decent clothes, no parties and no Ben, just when she was getting somewhere with him? But the long-awaited visit from her best friend, Joanne, brings some unexpected conflicts and Sally finds her determination to remain apart slowly undermined by the presence of a boy called Danny . . .

Love, Emma £1.25

Emma begins her nursing training with high hopes. Determined to achieve something for herself, she still finds the three-year separation from her established world of family and friends a little frightening. In letters to her parents, best friend and boyfriend – and in entries in her secret diary – Emma describes her new world in warm and witty detail . . . hard-working, occasionally exciting and always exhausting – but there are rewards; *and* a student doctor named Luke . . .

All Pan books are available at your local bookshop or newsagent, or can be ordered direct from the publisher. Indicate the number of copies required and fill in the form below.

Send to: **CS Department, Pan Books Ltd., P.O. Box 40, Basingstoke, Hants. RG21 2YT.**

or phone: 0256 469551 (Ansaphone), quoting title, author and Credit Card number.

Please enclose a remittance* to the value of the cover price plus: 60p for the first book plus 30p per copy for each additional book ordered to a maximum charge of £2.40 to cover postage and packing.

*Payment may be made in sterling by UK personal cheque, postal order, sterling draft or international money order, made payable to Pan Books Ltd.

Alternatively by Barclaycard/Access:

Card No.

Signature:

Applicable only in the UK and Republic of Ireland.

While every effort is made to keep prices low, it is sometimes necessary to increase prices at short notice. Pan Books reserve the right to show on covers and charge new retail prices which may differ from those advertised in the text or elsewhere.

NAME AND ADDRESS IN BLOCK LETTERS PLEASE:

Name

Address

3/87